To Kill For

A.J. Carella

PUBLISHED BY:

A.J. Carella

Copyright © 2014

This is a work of fiction. Names, characters, places, and incidents within are the product of the author's imagination or are used fictitiously, and any resemblance to actual persons, living or dead, business establishments, events, or location is entirely coincidental. The publisher does not have any control over and does not assume any responsibility for author or third-party websites or their content.

All rights reserved.

No part of this book may be reproduced, scanned, or distributed in any printed or electronic form without permission. Please do not participate in or encourage piracy of copyrighted materials in violation of the author's rights. Purchase only authorized editions.

One

What was she supposed to say? Every person in the room had their eyes glued to her, smiles on their faces. As Jamie glanced around at them all, she spotted her mom and dad. Dad had his arm around her mom's waist and both were beaming proudly as they looked at her, dressed in their finery. The invitations had been very clear. This was a black tie event and the guests were dressed up to the nines for this, her 21st birthday party.

As one of the wealthiest families in Brecon Point, entertaining was something they regularly did. For tonight's festivities, they'd taken over Faraday's Tennis Club, a place where you didn't usually get in unless you had a bank account in the seven figures. But tonight, just about everybody had been invited and social differences had been set aside. Now they were all standing around, looking at her.

As she peered down at the young man kneeling on one knee in front of her, Jamie was hit by a sudden wave of panic. She loved him. Well, she thought she did but she was only 21, far too young to get married. But what was she supposed to say? If she said no her parents would be devastated, not to mention completely embarrassed in front of all their guests.

He was starting to look a bit uncomfortable now and, with a jolt, Jamie realized that at least a full minute had passed since he'd presented her with the ring and asked her to marry him. She'd not said a word.

"Yes. Yes, of course I'll marry you." *What else could she say?*

***

Ted hadn't left her side since he'd slipped the ring on her finger. She had to admit, it was stunning and undoubtedly expensive, a cabochon cut yellow diamond, which fit perfectly on her left hand and flashed every time it caught the light. For the past hour, people had come up to them, shaking Ted's hand and admiring the ring. It was gorgeous. Ted was gorgeous. So why did she feel as though she'd just been put on a leash?

Ted Coleman, one of the Kentucky Colemans no less, had set his sights on her when she'd still been in high school. They'd met at one of the many social functions both their families had attended on one of his visits home from college and they'd started dating straight away. It had become serious once he had returned home and gone to work for his father. Her parents had been thrilled. He was from a good family and had excellent prospects, things that were still important to them, even in this day and age. Jamie knew they'd harbored hopes that the two of them would marry one day, but tonight's proposal had completely taken her by surprise.

"Did you know about this?" she whispered to her mom after finally giving Ted the slip for five minutes.

"Of course, darling. Ted came to see your father last week and asked for his permission." She beamed. "Isn't it wonderful? I'm thrilled for you both!"

"I guess." Jamie shrugged.

Her mom placed a hand on her arm. "Aren't you happy?"

Jamie looked into her mother's face and saw the question there. Not wanting to upset her, she forced herself to smile widely. "Of course I am, Mom. Still just a little shocked, I think."

Her mom wouldn't understand. She'd married her father at about the same age as Jamie was now. Theirs hadn't been a marriage of love, but more of an agreement between two families that it would be a good match. Not that they'd been unhappy, not at all. But her mom had taken on the role of good little wife, subservient to her husband, and that was not something Jamie had ever envisioned for herself. She wanted more out of life, wanted to see the world.

"Oh, good! Don't worry me like that!"

"Sorry, Mom." Jamie looked around. "Where's Jake? I haven't seen him since we got here."

"I don't know, darling. I saw him go outside with that Parker girl." She sniffed with distaste. "I just don't know what he sees in her."

Jamie knew exactly what her brother saw in her, but she didn't think it was something she should share with her mom. She loved her mother to pieces but she was a complete snob in some ways and Carrie Parker did not fit with what she had in mind for her only son.

"There you are!" a voice boomed, and Jamie turned to find Ted standing behind her. "Come on, my parents want to see the ring." Taking her by the elbow and making his apologies to her mother, he led her away.

Two

"Come on, baby." Jake pushed his hand up under Carrie's dress. The lights from the party shone on the bench where they were sitting and the sound of music and laughter drifted out across the lawn.

"Not here. Someone will see!" With a giggle, Carrie took him by the hand and led him away from the main club house and into a stand of trees a couple of hundred yards away.

Pushing her up against a tree he pressed himself against her, his hand once again lifting the hem of her dress.

"Careful! I saved up for ages to buy this!" she squeaked as he pushed her against the rough bark.

He didn't know why she'd bothered. The dress looked cheap, just like she did. Which was just the way he liked her.

"Well, there's one way to deal with that." he told her, reaching up behind her and undoing her zipper. Tugging the dress from her shoulders, it slithered to the ground with nothing left to keep it up. *That was more like it!* he thought to himself, as he looked her over, naked except for a tiny black thong.

She was an attractive girl, not classically beautiful, but not bad. Her light blonde hair with natural waves hung down to her shoulders and her eyes, wide like a doe's, were dark brown. It was her body, though, that was her best feature. He took it all in by the moonlight, her body slim and firm, with large perky breasts. The fact that she was always willing was what kept him coming back for more though. That's why he'd brought her to his sister's party tonight. He'd known full well that he would need his own entertainment and, looking at her now, he was glad he had.

***

"You do love me, don't you?" she asked him, as he was closing his zipper.

Here we go. "Would I have invited you tonight if I didn't?"

He avoided the question. It was not that he didn't *like* her but, let's face it, she wasn't wife material. She was the kind of girl you kept hidden away in an apartment somewhere to satisfy your needs at the drop of a hat. No, any wife of his would have breeding. And more importantly, money. His father had instilled that in him from a very early age.

He supposed he'd better go and show his face at the party or his parents would have his hide. He didn't want to give them yet another reason to remind him about how damned perfect his sister was.

She wasn't his biological sister. His parents had adopted him as a three-month-old, after years of trying to have children of their own. What they hadn't expected when they'd brought him home was to find out that, in a twist of fate, his mom had already been pregnant with his sister. Jamie had been born six months later.

He'd found out the truth shortly after his sixth birthday and he hadn't taken it well. His mom had since told him that she'd thought it was too soon, that he'd been too young, but his father had been insistent, telling her that it would toughen him up.

They'd sat him down and explained that his parents hadn't been able to take care of him properly so they'd chosen him to be theirs. Looking back, he knew that was when the first stirrings of discontent had settled within him, but it wasn't until later that these formed into something more.

He'd found out years later that his biological parents, whoever they were, had, in fact, abandoned him in a basket by the side of the road, unwanted and discarded like trash.

It was that knowledge more than anything else that had changed him then, that had sown the seed of the deep insecurity that had grown within him and fuelled his desire to be someone.

Ever since that day, he'd watched for signs that they preferred Jamie to him and he'd seen them everywhere, especially the way they'd look at him, disappointed, when Jamie brought home achievement award after achievement award from school and all he'd brought home were detention notices. Then, as they'd gotten older, she'd made friends with all the *right* people while his friends were frowned upon.

And now, tonight. Yet again, Jamie had lived up to their dreams of the perfect child and gotten engaged to the perfect man. When his parents had told him what was going to happen tonight, he'd been determined not to be there. He didn't think he could face seeing their disappointment in him yet again. He was finding it harder and harder these days to hide his feelings.

Pushing open the French doors to where the party was in full swing, he scanned the room. He saw that his mom had spotted him coming in with Carrie in tow and watched as a frown appeared on her face. Taking Carrie by the hand, he made his way over to her, weaving in and out of the partygoers until he was standing in front of her.

"Where've you been, Jake? You missed your sister's big moment," she asked, a hard edge to her voice.

"Did I? I'm sorry. I must have lost track of time," he replied innocently, controlling the smirk that threatened to appear on his lips. "What did she say?"

"What do you think she said? She said yes, of course."

"Of course." Yeah. *She wouldn't rock the boat and say anything else, would she?* he thought to himself.

His parents had come to have low expectations of him, but that was not the case where Jamie was concerned. In their eyes, her path was clear. Marry well and provide good stock. Jamie knew this and would never let them down, however much she may want to.

"Well, I think you need to go apologize." She looked pointedly at Carrie. "Alone."

Jake bridled. It didn't bother him in the slightest if Carrie was offended by his mother's obvious disdain, but he hated being told what to do like a naughty child. He had to play his cards right, though. He worked for his dad and he was angling for a promotion. The manufacturing firm that had made his family so wealthy had been founded by his great-great-grandfather on his mother's side and had grown over the generations. Now, it was one of the biggest firms in the southern United States.

"Go and get yourself a drink. I'll go and find Jamie and then I'll come and join you," he told Carrie, doing as he was told.

"I take it you're still involved with that girl?" his mother asked him as she watched her walk away.

"Involved is probably too strong a word. We're having some fun."

"Well, make sure that's all it is and that she doesn't get any ideas. And please, in the future, keep your sordid little dalliances away from family occasions." Her face softened. "I love you, darling. I only want what's best for you."

Jake nodded. "I know, Mom, don't worry."

He knew that it was true, that his mother did love him, but he couldn't help the simmering resentment he felt, resentment that just seemed to grow with every bit of praise they heaped on Jamie and every bit of criticism they aimed at him.

Searching the room, he spotted her in a corner, talking to one of their parents' friends.

"Can I interrupt? I understand congratulations are in order!" He smiled.

"Jake!" Jamie's face broke into a wide grin. Making her excuses to their parents' friend, she took him by the arm and led him to a quiet spot. "Did you know about this?"

"Sure did. Aren't you pleased?" He eyed her curiously. He loved his sister and despite resenting the praise that was heaped on her, he knew it wasn't her fault. Being so similar in age, they'd been very close growing up and she'd often run interference with his father when she could see him coming down hard on him.

"Well, yes, I suppose I am, but it would have been nice to have been warned!"

"I was sworn to secrecy!" He held up his hands in mock surrender.

Playfully, she punched him in the arm. "Since when have you been able to keep a secret?"

She had a point. Growing up, there had been many times when she'd asked him to keep a secret from their parents. Nothing serious, usual kid stuff, but he'd never been able to, always running straight to them to share what he knew. He realized now that this was his way of trying to gain his parents' approval, particularly his father's, rather than any attempt at getting her into trouble. It was as if Jamie had known this, though, and she'd never been angry with him.

"Well, I hope you'll both be very happy," he said, which was true. He didn't want her to be unhappy.

"Thank you, Jake. That means a lot." She smiled at him now, a twinkle in her eye. "So, where were you? I couldn't see you?"

"Sorry, Jamie, I didn't mean to miss it." He felt a twinge of guilt as he lied to her, but he hadn't done it to hurt her.

"Are you and Carrie serious, then?" she asked knowingly.

"God, no!"

"So, why did you bring her as your date tonight?" she sighed. "You know what Mom and Dad are like. You're only making things harder for yourself."

He knew she was right, but he increasingly felt the need to push the boundaries.

"Dad's never going to promote you unless you show him you can tow the party line, you know that." She put her hand on the sleeve of his jacket. "Just try, for me?"

She was right, of course. His father was very old fashioned in his views. Men could and should be men, but they should keep it discreet and always go back to their wives at the end of the night. His being so open about his relationship with Carrie, a girl very much from the wrong side of the tracks, was proving a real bone of contention between them. His father didn't mind that he was sleeping with her, but he didn't want all their friends to know about it.

Covering her hand with his own, he smiled. "Okay, just for you."

"Where is the lucky man, anyway?" he asked, scanning the room.

"Oh, he won't be far away. He's hardly left my side all night." She turned and had a quick look, too. "He's over there, at the bar."

He turned to look and sure enough, he was there, talking to Carrie. "I'd better go and take her home before Mom and dad disown me."

Jamie chuckled. "Come on, they're not bad."

He just looked at her and raised his eyebrow. "You and I both know that they are!"

"Yeah, you're right. They are!" She pushed him away gently. "Go on, take her home. I'll see you tomorrow."

Still chuckling, he made his way over to the bar where Ted and Carrie were still talking. It wasn't until he got closer that he realized, from the expression on their faces and the way that they were trying to keep their voices down, that they were having a disagreement.

"I've already told you no!"

"Am I interrupting anything?" Jake asked curiously as he joined them. "What have you said no to?" he asked, turning his gaze to Ted, who now looked like he'd been caught with his hand in the cookie jar.

"Nothing. Nothing at all." With a glare at Carrie, Ted turned and stalked off.

"What was that about?"

"Oh, it really was nothing."

He didn't believe her for a second. "Tell me."

"Really! I was just getting a bit pushy about getting him to buy me a drink, that's all." She couldn't meet his eyes.

There was no doubt in his mind as he looked at her that she was lying, but he didn't know why. "Come on. I'm taking you home."

Grabbing their coats from the cloakroom, they made their way out to his car.

"Your mom looked absolutely thrilled to see me," she said sarcastically, turning to him as he started the car.

"Don't start, Carrie. You know what they're like." They'd had this conversation many times before.

"I just wish you'd stand up for me now and then. It wouldn't kill you, especially if you really love me," she pouted.

The sex was great, and pissing off his folks was a bonus, but maybe it was time to think about ditching her. Her whining was starting to get on his nerves.

Reaching across the seat, she pressed her hand to his crotch. "You gonna stay for a while when we get to my place?"

Maybe I can put up with her just a little longer. He smiled. "Yeah, why not."

Three

Ted watched as Jamie chatted to some of her guests in a corner of the room. She was pretty enough, there was no doubt about that, but she really didn't do it for him. For a start, she wasn't a blonde and though slim, she was far too curvy for his tastes. He like his women stick thin, blonde and with huge breasts. And preferably without too much in the brains department. But she had one thing going for her. Money. Tons of it. And when her parents died, it would come to her.

The Colemans came from old money and mixed with the upper echelons of society, but what was kept as a closely guarded family secret was that the money had almost completely run out. Through a series of bad investments and worse business decisions, his father had managed to pretty much decimate the entire family fortune, leaving them mere months away from complete financial ruin.

The idea of courting Jamie had been his parents'. They'd come up with the idea after seeing her at one of the many dinner parties they attended, and it had struck them as the perfect solution to their problems. Once they'd sat him down and explained about the business and how they faced losing everything, he hadn't needed much persuasion.

The idea of poverty sickened him. He was used to the finer things in life and he intended to keep them. He had no intention of giving up his way of life, if he could help it. And it wasn't so bad. She was nice enough, and it wasn't going to get in the way of what he really enjoyed. Knocking back the last of his drink, he made his way over to them.

"Darling, I'm so sorry, but I have to go and take care of a problem at work," he said, putting his arm around her waist. "Would you be able to get a ride home with your mom and dad?" He had the sudden urge to get out of there and away from all the well-wishers.

"Really? It can't wait?" she asked.

"No. I'm sorry, darling, but I really need to go and take care of this." Working for his dad in the company's IT department, he was frequently called out at strange hours, so she accepted his explanation readily. "We're having lunch with your parents tomorrow at the house, so I'll see you there."

Leaning down, he briefly pressed his lips to hers. "Thank you for saying 'yes', my darling. I'm the happiest man on earth right now."

Maybe I should have gone into acting! he thought, as he turned and walked to the exit, his steps quickening. He'd done his duty tonight and now he was looking forward to taking care of a bit of personal business.

***

He drove faster than was sensible on the unlit roads after leaving the party. The run-in with Carrie had unnerved him more than he'd like to admit. He'd managed to avoid her for the last few months and it had been a surprise to see her there tonight. He'd had no idea she now had Jake McKay in her sites. Well, good luck to him. *He's gonna need it!*

He was still angry at himself for his relationship with Carrie. She worked in the diner in town and they'd met over a year ago by chance while she'd been at work and he'd gone in on one of his trips home. They'd flirted a bit, and she was exactly his type, but he'd been interested enough to give her his number. They'd met up the next day and she'd taken him back to her place. The sex had damn near blown his mind.

He'd never intended for it to go any further. He'd already been dating Jamie by then, but he'd kept going back for more. What he hadn't bargained on was that Carrie would see him as her meal ticket, becoming more and more demanding over time.

In the end he'd had no choice, he'd already risked too much as it was, so he ended it. She hadn't taken it well, and he'd suffered months of phone calls and visits before she'd finally backed off. *Now he knew why!*

She'd asked him again tonight if he wanted to resume their affair, and she'd gotten quite upset when he'd refused. He just hoped that seeing him tonight didn't set her off again.

He was nearly there, now. The house he was visiting was in the next town over, down a street filled with run down houses that all looked exactly the same. He'd learned his lesson with Carrie and would never play so close to home again, so this time he'd been careful to go further afield. He parked his car about a block away and walked back, not wanting to be seen. It was unlikely that anyone here would recognize him, but he wasn't taking any chances.

The house he was visiting was slightly more cared for than the others, and there were indications of someone trying to make it nice. The yard in the front had been mowed and planted and the porch was tidy, though the paint was still peeling from the wooden bannister.

The door opened before he even got to the top of the steps. Silhouetted by the light coming from behind her was his idea of the perfect woman. About five foot eight with long, platinum blonde hair, the outline of her slim body was clearly visible through her flimsy robe.

"Where've you been, honey? I've been waiting for you," she purred at him, stepping aside so he could enter the house.

Closing the door behind him, she turned and leaned against the door, looking at him from under her eyelashes. "I missed you."

Without a word, he pulled her to him, crushing her lips with his own, his hands snaking around her to pull her tight against him.

***

It took a few minutes for him to get his breath back and he stayed on the couch as Carla went to fix them a drink, slipping her robe back on as she went. He felt better now, more relaxed. He'd been visiting Carla for about six months, several times a week. It suited them both. She was quite a bit older than he was, in her late thirties, but she looked much younger and certainly had the body of a younger woman.

Perhaps because there were no expectations of him, he felt comfortable here, with her. She was twice divorced and had no intentions of getting into a serious relationship again. She'd made that clear from the start. That suited him, too,.

Sex with Jamie wasn't something that he spent much time thinking about. She had very little effect on him in that department. He quite simply didn't find her attractive. It was a shame, considering he was marrying her, but as long as he had Carla, or someone like her, he would manage.

"So, how was the party? You all engaged now to little Miss Moneybags?" she asked as she brought their drinks and sat down next to him. He'd told her all about it and she teased him mercilessly.

"Yep, I am now officially a soon-to-be-married man." He raised his glass in a mock toast.

"Pleased?" She smiled as she brought her glass to her lips.

"Don't, Carla. You know I'm only doing it because I have to."

"I know, sweetie. I'm only messing with you. As long as I still get to share you, you know I'm happy." She pressed a kiss to his lips.

"You're the thing that's going to keep me sane."

"Where does she think you are?"

"I told her I had some business to take care of." Putting his glass on the coffee table, he turned back to her and pushed her robe off her shoulders once more. "So, I think I'd better take care of it. Again."

***

The ride back home after the party seemed like it had taken forever. Ted had gone to take care of God knows what and Jake had gone off with Carrie, probably for the night. That had left her alone with her folks.

It wasn't a long drive from the tennis club, fifteen minutes at most, but it had certainly felt longer. Her mother was so excited to have a wedding to plan that she hadn't stopped chattering the whole way. Jamie had been pleased when they'd arrived home and she'd been able to make her excuses and escape to her room for some peace and quiet.

Her room was at the back of the house, overlooking the gardens. Pushing open the doors to her private balcony, she breathed in the night air and enjoyed the stillness after the noise of the evening.

The proposal had taken her by surprise, but what had surprised her even more had been her reaction to it. There was no denying it, her first instinct had been to panic. *But why?* She needed to understand. *Was she excited?* She wasn't quite sure what she was if she was honest with herself. Pleased? Yes. Excited? No, she didn't think so. She should be though, right? *Probably just hasn't sunk in yet*, she told herself.

This really wasn't the direction she'd seen her life taking. She had done really well at school, had been a straight A student and had gotten in to the college of her choice, studying business. She'd always had an aptitude for numbers, so she'd thought she might go to graduate school and do something in that field. Exactly what she didn't know, but that was part of the excitement, having her whole future ahead of her and getting to make those choices.

Just because you're getting married doesn't mean that you can't follow your dream. Does it? Would she still be able to go to school and do all the things she wanted to do?

The chill in the air was starting to seep through her clothes now, and she was feeling cold. Stepping back into her bedroom, she closed the balcony doors behind her and pulled the drapes.

Sitting down at her dresser to remove her make-up, she looked at herself in the mirror. She wasn't unattractive, but not quite beautiful. Her dark brown hair was waist length and naturally wavy; her best feature, she thought. Her amber-colored eyes were fringed by long, dark lashes and their shape was slightly cat-like. She'd inherited her father's nose though, masculine and angular and to her mind, it jarred with the rest of her face.

Ted, on the other hand, was gorgeous and she knew that she should be grateful that he wanted to marry her when he could have his pick of any woman in the state. On top of that, her parents were thrilled and she loved her parents. She could no more disappoint them than stick pins in her own eyes.

There was no doubt about it, she was very lucky. She had always had everything she'd ever asked for and her parents treated her like a princess.

It came at a price, though. As a McKay, she knew what was expected of her: a good marriage and babies, most definitely in that order. She hadn't broached the subject of grad school with them yet, knowing full well what her father's reaction would be. He saw no point in women getting an expensive education that, in his mind, they wouldn't need. He'd paid for college and was now supporting her with an allowance, and he was happy to do it until her future husband took on the role, but it was not what she wanted. She wanted to be able to provide for herself, to stand on her own two feet.

Unfortunately, she knew that she was going to have a battle on her hands when she finally did screw up the courage to tell her folks of her plans. *So why on earth did you say yes?* Because she was a good, dutiful daughter. Besides, she was only *engaged* to be married. There was no reason it couldn't be a long engagement, was there?

Getting undressed and ready for bed, she resolved to talk to Ted tomorrow. A long engagement seemed like the perfect solution. Once she'd convinced him, she would talk to her parents about her plans. She'd been putting it off for too long.

Four

The McKay house sat on the outskirts of Brecon Point on several acres of land. It was a typical, two-storey colonial style house, though much larger than most.

The long, stately driveway to the house from the main road was lined with tall trees, meeting overhead to leave it covered in dappled shade. In the summer months the effect was pretty, but in winter, it had an air of gloom about it. Once free of the trees, the driveway led to a large turning circle in front of the imposing front door.

Inside, the ceilings were high and in the center of each room hung a crystal chandelier. The interior décor was in keeping with the style of the house, and at the same time light and airy. A large, spiral staircase led up to the second floor from the main hall and it was down this that Jake now made his way from his room. He'd been at work all morning and had just freshened up before lunch.

Normally, they each went about their own business and rarely saw each other during the day. His mom was the typical society wife, on the boards of a large number of charitable foundations. She was always busy rushing around from one luncheon to the next and it was almost unheard of for his dad to be home in the middle of a workday. Today, though, they were all meeting in the formal dining room at one o'clock, including Ted and his parents, to celebrate the engagement.

As Jake approached the door, he could tell from the voices that everybody had already arrived. He would have gotten out of it if he could but he was already in trouble for missing the proposal yesterday. He didn't dare push his luck. The idea of sitting around a table talking weddings filled him with dread but it was for his sister so, taking a deep breath and putting a smile on his face, he opened the door and made his way into the room.

The formal dining room was rarely used but today the table, capable of seating sixteen, had been laid with the best silverware and china. Colorful floral centerpieces had been placed in lovely arrangements at the center at regular intervals.

"Afternoon, all," he greeted them, taking his usual seat at the table to the right of his father.

For the next hour as the different courses of lunch were served, the conversation flowed over a variety of topics, from the weather to the local economy.

When they'd all finished eating and the plates had been removed, his father cleared his throat and stood up.

"My wife and I are absolutely thrilled that our two great families are to be joined together."

Jake held in a groan as he watched his dad beam at Jamie and Ted across the table. "I know that they haven't set a date yet, but we would like to give them one of our wedding presents early." He turned to Ted. "How would you like to come and work for me and head up a section of our IT department? It would mean taking on a supervisory role and obviously comes with a bigger salary than you have at the moment."

What the hell? Jake felt everything slip into slow motion and there was a loud rushing noise in his ears, like the pounding of a waterfall.

"I don't know what to say!" Ted seemed genuinely surprised. "I'd have to speak to my dad. As you know, I work for him." He looked across the table at his father, who seemed equally surprised.

"It's fine with me, son, if that's what you want," he said graciously.

"I'd be honoured then, sir. Thank you." He watched as Ted, beaming, stood up and shook his father's hand.

Jake tried to keep his cool, but failed. The rushing noise in his ears was closing in on him, getting louder and more intense. Pushing back his chair with a screech and throwing down his napkin, he stormed out of the room. The sound of congratulations and laughter that followed him made him even angrier. *He'd been promised that job for months!*

Leaning one arm against the wall in the hallway, he bent over and rested his hand on his knee. Breathing deeply, he tried to push away the storm in his head. A hand on his shoulder made him jerk away and he turned, ready to lay into whoever it was. Jamie stood there, her eyes wide pools of concern.

"Are you okay?"

He didn't trust himself to answer, so he just shook his head and concentrated on his breathing.

"Come back in. Please."

"It's just like my birthday, isn't it?" he said, when he found his voice at last. "The bastard's done it yet again."

When he'd been fifteen, all he'd wanted for his sixteenth birthday had been a car. He dreamed about it, about the freedom it would give him and how, for once in his life, he would get something that Jamie didn't already have as she wouldn't be old enough to drive until six months later.

There had been a big test coming up at school and his dad had promised him that if he did well, he would get him a car. Used to skipping school and getting bad grades, Jake had put a huge amount of effort in, studying every night and working damned hard. He knew the minute he'd finished the test that he'd done well, and it had been confirmed a couple of weeks later when he'd come home with a B-, thrilled. He'd proudly presented the paper to his father, who had merely nodded and walked away.

It didn't matter. Jake knew he'd done well and on the morning of his birthday he'd woken up at the crack of dawn, so excited he couldn't stay in bed any longer.

He'd waited all day but the car never materialized. A couple of days later, he'd come home to find a shiny new BMW sitting in the driveway in front of the house. He'd rushed inside, almost bursting with excitement. Finding his father in his office, he'd gone to hug him, to thank him, only to be told that the car was for Jamie. Only six months apart in age, they'd taken the same test. She'd got an A+. It made no difference to his father that he'd made a promise, that Jake had worked so very hard and, for him, had done incredibly well.

He hadn't been able to stop himself bursting into tears in front of him, tears that his father had looked upon with disdain before walking away and leaving him to his crushing disappointment.

He'd had to look at that car every day for the next six months, idle in the driveway, until Jamie had gotten her license. She'd been distraught seeing what their father had done and hadn't wanted the car, but he had insisted. She'd done what she could, though, and every morning, just after leaving for school, she'd pulled that car over and swapped places with him and for the day, at least, it had been his.

All those feelings were back now, overwhelming him. Furious, he grabbed his car keys and jacket and stormed out of the front door. His black, convertible Mercedes was parked out front and he jumped in. The door was barely closed before he put his foot to the floor and drove off down the drive, wheels squealing and leaving a dust cloud in the air.

***

Jamie was furious with her dad. Could he really not see what he had done to Jake? How much he had hurt him? If he really wanted to give Ted a job, he could have given him any job. Why the one he'd promised to Jake? She walked back into the dining room just as her dad was asking Ted a question.

"So, have you set a date yet?"

Jamie opened her mouth to speak but before she could, Ted answered.

"Well, Jamie doesn't know this, but I've got a surprise." He was grinning widely at her as she stood in the doorway.

"What do you mean?" Returning to her seat, she wasn't sure she wanted to know the answer.

"Well, I knew you'd been as anxious as I am to get married as quickly as possible, so I've already booked the church. It's all set for two months from today!"

He seemed thrilled with himself as he looked around the table at their parents. They seemed thrilled, too. Her mom was clapping her hands together excitedly and her dad beamed. His parents, though, while looking pleased didn't look at all surprised.

"What do you mean you've already booked the church?" Jamie said quietly, not quite trusting her voice.

"Yes! Isn't it wonderful, darling?" Ted took her hands in his and squeezed.

She pulled her hands away sharply. "You're joking, aren't you?" Her voice was getting louder now. "Please tell me you're joking!"

He looked confused now. "I thought you'd be pleased."

"You're just going to have to cancel it." She glared at him, daring him to argue. *What on earth was he thinking?*

"Err...I think we'll leave you kids to talk." It was her dad. She was so angry she had almost forgotten that he was there. She waited until the others had left the room before speaking again.

"How could you do this without even talking to me? And I could have said 'no' for all you knew!"

He smiled indulgently. "Come on, Jamie, we both know you weren't going to say no."

Oh really? "You think you know me that well, do you?" She was getting angrier by the minute. *How dare he!*

"I know I love you and that you love me." Once again he took her hands in his own and looked into her eyes. "And I know that we want to be together forever." *Dammit!* He knew exactly what buttons to push.

Her anger was dissolving now. "But I've got so many things I want to do before I get married. I was going to talk to you today. At the very least, I want to go to grad school!"

He nodded. "I know, darling, and I certainly won't stop you."

"So why can't we wait? What's the rush?"

"I just don't think I could wait for you unless I knew you were coming back to me."

"Are you actually saying that if I don't marry you before I go to school, if I go, you'll find someone else?"

"No, I'm saying that it would be hard to hold onto something that you obviously don't want as much as I do."

There it was, then. Her choice. Get married now or lose him, and she didn't want to lose him. Quite aside from the fact that her parents would never forgive her, eligible bachelors weren't exactly beating a path to her door.

For the second time in as many days, she found herself agreeing to something that she wasn't sure about but didn't have the strength to refuse.

Five

"We've got so much to organize, darling!" Jamie groaned as her mother wafted into her bedroom on a cloud of perfume, waving a pen and pad in the air.

"We've got to organize the wedding planner, the dress, the flowers...oh, God, where do we start?"

"Mom. It's 7:30 in the morning. Can I at least get up and have some breakfast first?"

Her mom seemed to realize only then that her daughter had been sleeping soundly until she'd burst into the room.

"Yes, darling, of course. I'm sorry. I'm just so excited!"

Jamie smiled indulgently. "I am too, Mom. I'll see you downstairs in a bit, okay?" Sighing, she dropped back onto her pillows as her mom left the room. She knew she didn't want to lose Ted, so she'd made the only decision left to if she wanted to keep him. And, after all, it was what she wanted. Just a bit sooner than she'd planned.

As soon as she'd agreed to the date, they'd told her parents the good news. It didn't give them long to get everything organized, so it had sent her mom into a whirlwind of frantic activity. It was only on the promise that she would spend the morning with her today that she'd been allowed to escape to her bedroom for some sleep at nearly midnight last night.

In her en-suite bathroom, she took a quick shower and threw on some blue jeans and a white t-shirt. Not bothering to blow dry her hair, she pinned it up on top of her head and went downstairs to have breakfast. She would need fortifying. It sounded like her mom had a busy day planned for her.

She was just coming down the stairs when a dishevelled Jake walked through the front door. Taking one look at him, she knew he'd been out all night. He was still wearing the same clothes he'd been wearing at lunch the day before.

"You okay?" she asked. She'd been worried about him since he'd stormed out the day before.

"Yeah, fine," he mumbled, although it was clear from his face that he was, in fact, far from fine.

"Look, why don't you talk to Dad again?" she replied gently.

"I shouldn't have to beg my own father for a job that he'd already promised me, that's why." He brushed past her and up the stairs but paused, turning to look at her. "I'm sorry. It's not your fault. I shouldn't take it out on you."

"Do you want me to talk to him?"

"Thank you, but no. It's my problem."

Jamie watched as he walked upstairs. Her father was harder on him than he was on her but, unlike Jake, she didn't think it had anything to do with being adopted. Her dad was old school and firmly believed that the men should be tough and women should be cherished.

A memory flashed into her mind then of when they were both eight years old. They'd been playing in the yard and Jake had started climbing a tree. He'd been halfway up when he'd slipped and fallen.

Jamie could still remember the way his arm had looked, with the bone snapped and sticking out through his skin, gleaming white in the sun. She'd run back to the house to get her mom but she'd bumped into her dad first. Hysterical, she told him what had happened and he followed her out to where Jake lay sobbing on the ground, clutching his arm to his chest and screaming in pain.

It still broke her heart and made her eyes fill up when she thought of what had happened next. Offering him no comfort, her dad had told him that he would take him to the hospital, but only when he stopped crying, that no son of his was going to embarrass him by behaving like a girl.

He made him sit there, in excruciating pain, for nearly an hour before he took him for help.

Brushing the memory away, she turned her thoughts back to the day ahead.

***

Freedom! She'd finally managed to escape her mother's clutches and was now looking forward to spending a nice afternoon with Ted. Since the engagement, they hadn't spent any time alone together at all, really. She'd spent the last couple of hours with her mom going through endless bridal magazines and looking at pictures of celebrity weddings. Her mom seemed thrilled to have a project to work on and Jamie suspected that her life wasn't going to be her own again until after the wedding. She would be quite happy with a simple service at the local church, but she wasn't naïve enough to think that that was an option. She loved her mom to absolute pieces, but when it came to social events, she'd never understood her passion for everything having to be bigger and better. She'd left her on the phone to the wedding planner, happily organizing, and was making her getaway before she changed her mind!

The last couple of days had been a bit of a blur with her birthday party, the proposal and now being hit with wedding plans all of a sudden. It was nice to be able to clear her head and put it all out of her mind as she drove over to Ted's place. He'd offered to come and get her, but she loved driving and had relished the idea of a bit of time on her own. She sure couldn't get any peace at home at the moment.

Ted had his own place on the edge of town. The town itself was not very big, home to only about twenty-five thousand residents, most of who worked in her father's manufacturing plant, which underpinned the local economy. Those who didn't either worked for Ted's family or commuted to other, larger towns nearby.

His house wasn't huge and didn't need to be, as he lived there on his own, but it was nonetheless impressive. The two-storey house was comfortable, and she pondered the fact that it was where she would soon live, seeing it with new eyes.

The ground floor was split between the kitchen, living room, entertainment room and bathroom. They all contained the latest electronic gadgets and the entertainment room featured a sunken area in the center of the room filled with couches and a movie screen that took up an entire wall.

The whole top floor was dedicated to a single bedroom and bath, the highlight of which was the glass panels in the ceiling, allowing the room to be flooded with light.

Jamie had only seen the bedroom, she'd never stayed there. She firmly believed in no sex before marriage, much to the amusement of all her friends, and was still a virgin. Sure, she'd fooled around some but she'd never gone too far. Ted had been wonderful about it, completely understanding and accepting her beliefs, though she knew that it must be hard for him sometimes.

Parking outside the house, she switched off the car engine and got out. Letting herself in, she found Ted in the kitchen.

"Have you eaten?" he asked, turning to her as she walked in.

She shook her head.

"Good, I'm just making us a salad." She watched as he chopped tomatoes and tossed them into a bowl.

She didn't know why she was having these nagging doubts about marrying him. He'd never given her any reason to feel this way. In fact, the opposite was true. He treated her wonderfully and really did make her happy. But she couldn't help but feel that something was missing. A spark maybe.

On the occasions where they had indulged in some fairly heavy fooling around, she'd never felt disappointed when she'd had to put an end to it. She had nothing to compare it to, but from listening to her girlfriends, she knew that this wasn't the way it should be.

Maybe it was just her inexperience. It certainly wasn't his looks. At six feet tall, he towered over her five foot six frame. He couldn't be described as well built. Lanky was the word that sprang to mind. His hair was dark brown, almost black, and he wore it slightly long, showing its natural wave. He had the brownest eyes she had ever seen.

Pushing the negative thoughts aside, she went up to him and slid her arms around his waist, resting her cheek on his back.

"I do love you, you know, and I can't wait to be Mrs. Ted Coleman," she whispered.

Putting the knife down, he turned and wrapped her in his arms. "And I love you," he said, resting his chin on top of her head.

***

Ted was quite pleased with himself. Everything was going perfectly, exactly according to plan. He knew full well that Jamie didn't want to get married so soon, but his father's business was on the brink of collapse and he couldn't afford to wait.

He'd known that getting Jamie to do what he wanted wouldn't be hard. She was so damn eager to please all the time. All it took was a little bit of pressure, a bit of emotional blackmail and she was like putty in his hands. It helped that her parents were completely on board. He knew there was no way she'd let them down.

As soon as they'd tied the knot, he would find a way to divert some much needed funds. Being given the job was a bonus he hadn't counted on and it would make things a lot easier.

"Is your brother okay? He looked really upset yesterday."

She sighed into his chest. "Yeah, he'll be okay. He's pissed with dad."

"Anything I can do?" He didn't care in the slightest but it was always good to show concern.

"That's why I love you." She smiled up at him. "You're so thoughtful."

He reached down and kissed her. "Okay, come on and sit down. Let's eat, and then we can have a nice afternoon, just you and me, curled up on the couch watching a movie. And I promise, no talk of weddings."

She laughed softly. "Deal."

Six

His father was due home from work any minute, and Jake was determined to talk to him. They hadn't spoken since the announcement at lunch yesterday and he needed some answers.

Jake was sitting in his private office at the back of the house where it was quiet. He hated this room, but it was his father's favorite one in the house. To him it was far too dark and gloomy, but his father liked the dark wood paneling and bookshelves and the big old oak desk. The desk faced the full length French doors, which opened onto a private patio area.

Jake didn't know why he hated it so much but it may well be because, when they were kids, this was the room to which they'd be summoned when they were in trouble. If you were called to Dad's office, you knew you had a big problem.

But he wasn't a kid anymore and it was about time his father gave him some answers.

Jake jumped as the door opened. He hadn't heard him approach.

"What are you doing in here?" his father asked him, a frown on his face.

"Waiting for you, Dad. We need to talk."

"About your behavior yesterday? I'll say we do. It was a disgrace, and you embarrassed us in front of our guests." He closed the door behind him and went to sit behind his desk.

Jake sighed. "And why do you think that was?"

"Don't you dare give me any lip, Jake. If you've got something to say, say it."

"Okay, I will. You promised me that job months ago. It's what I've been working my ass off for." He tried to filter the anger out of his voice.

"It's my company and I'll give the job to who I damn well like. You're far too young for a management job, anyway."

"But it'll be my company someday. Surely that counts for something?"

"So because you're my son you should automatically have gotten the job?" he laughed. "Is that what you're saying?"

"Damn you, no! But I understood that's what I was working toward, that's what we agreed."

"Well, you'll just have to get over it, won't you?" He smiled. "And stop whining. You'll take what you're given and be grateful for it."

All the frustration, the anger and the bitterness boiled over then. "Yeah, that's exactly it, isn't it? I'm not your real son so I should be grateful for every scrap you hand me? That's what you're really saying, isn't it?" he shouted.

"Stop being so pathetic. Even if you were my biological son, I would be saying exactly the same thing."

"So, you admit you don't think of me as your son?"

"Now you're putting words in my mouth."

"Come on, admit it. You've never thought of me in the same way as Jamie, have you? You've always thought of me as an outsider."

"I am not having this conversation." He started taking papers out of his briefcase and Jake recognized the signal that, as far as he was concerned, it was the end of the discussion.

"No, because that would mean admitting your true feelings, wouldn't it?" Angrily, he pushed himself to his feet and turned to leave. As he had his hand on the door handle, his father stopped him.

"One more thing, Jake. As you don't seem to appreciate everything I do, and have done for you, consider yourself fired."

Without a word Jake walked out of the office, slamming the door behind him and storming down the hall. *Bastard!*

What was he supposed to do now? Get a job at the local McDonalds? It was not as if there were many decent opportunities around here and there was no way he was going to be turned into the local laughing stock by doing something menial, not when his father was the richest man for miles.

But with no job, what was he supposed to do for money? Unlike Jamie, everything he had, he paid for himself. Even his car was financed. He'd have to give that up for a start.

No way was he going to let that happen. He'd just have to think of something, and fast.

***

Feeling her hand stroking him through his pants, Jake smiled. He'd needed some light relief and Carrie was just the girl to give it to him.

"You need to stop that or I'm going to have to pull over and nail you right here," he laughed, removing her hand from his lap.

He'd just picked her up and was on the main road back into town. The plan was to hit the local bar and drink as much as he could before going back to her place and screwing her brains out. He hoped that might put thoughts of his damn family out of his mind for a few hours.

As he turned his attention back to the road, he was passed by a red Porsche traveling in the opposite direction. *There weren't two cars like that in town!* Checking the clock on his dash, he saw that it was nearly 11 p.m. Where was Ted going at this time of night? His house was two miles out of town in the opposite direction.

With his curiosity piqued, he swung his car around and started following him from a distance.

"Hey! I thought we were heading into town?" Carrie protested.

"We are, there's just something I need to do first."

"Is that Ted Coleman's car?"

"It sure is. And I'm wondering where he could be going at this time of night."

"What on earth for? He could be going anywhere."

"True, but it would be interesting to see."

They followed him for the next ten miles, hanging back as the roads were quiet and he didn't want to be spotted, before Ted took the turn-off toward Duke. Duke was a small town and it didn't take long for Ted to get where he was going. Confused, Jake stopped a few cars behind him and watched as he got out of his car and crossed the street. He walked past several houses before turning a corner and Jake had to pull the car forward to be able to see down the next street, just in time to see Ted walk up to a run-down old house. As he watched, light spilled out onto the porch as the door was opened by a woman wearing a short robe and a smile. *What the hell?* She'd clearly been expecting him, and opened the door and let him in, closing it behind him.

"Wait here!" he told Carrie, checking his jacket pocket to make sure he had his phone.

"Why? Where are you going?"

"To see what he's up to, of course. I have a feeling that this trip won't have been a waste of time."

Happy that his phone was there, he got out of the car and jogged across the street to the house where he'd seen Ted go in. It wasn't a big house and there was no gate blocking access to the back yard, so Jake disappeared down the side before anyone could spot him. There was light spilling from one of the side windows so, creeping closer and praying that he didn't make a noise, he carefully peered into the window.

What he saw made him grin. *Why, the dirty lying bastard!*

Ted wouldn't have noticed Jake even if he'd shined a flashlight in the window. He was sitting on a couch pushed back against the wall opposite the window with his head resting on the back of it, eyes closed. The woman he'd seen at the door was kneeling between his legs, 'entertaining' him.

Slipping the phone from his pocket, Jake took several pictures, checking each time to make sure you could see what was going on.

He stayed there for another ten minutes, taking several more pictures of Ted in increasingly passionate and compromising positions, before he was happy that he had enough.

Getting back to the car, he grinned widely as he slipped back behind the wheel.

"What are you so happy about?"

"Oh, you'll see, honey. You'll see."

***

Ted had never had much to do with Jamie's brother, so what little he knew of him, he knew from her. So it was a bit of a surprise when he got a call from Jake, asking him if he'd like to meet him for a beer. Actually, he could think of many things he would rather be doing but he couldn't afford to upset his fiancée's brother. Nothing could get in the way of this wedding. Nothing.

Jake had suggested a bar quite a ways out of town, and as he pulled into the parking lot he couldn't for the life of him think why. The bar was a one-story building, seemingly just dropped by the side of the road. There were no other buildings for miles, as far as he could tell. It looked run down and only a couple of the letters on the illuminated sign spelling out the bar's name actually worked.

There were only two other cars in the lot, both old, beat up pick-up trucks, and his Porsche seemed completely out of place. There was no sign of Jake's Mercedes yet and, checking his watch, he realized he was a few minutes early. They'd agreed to meet at 9 p.m. and it was just before that now.

Pushing open the door to the building, he was immediately assaulted by the smell of smoke and stale beer. Once his eyes had adjusted to the dull gloom, he surveyed the room, taking in the old battered tables, the filthy floor and the yellowed lights. *The beer must be fantastic,* he thought to himself wryly. Why else would he have suggested this dump?

He'd just sat on a stool and ordered a beer from the very disinterested-looking bartender when Jake walked in.

"Beer?" he asked, as he stood up and shook his hand.

Jake nodded. "Yeah, that would be good. Shall I grab us a table?"

Ted nodded, waiting and then paying for the beers before following him over to a table in the corner of the room. There were no mats and the table was sticky as he put the glasses down. God, he hoped he could wrap this up quickly and get out of this shithole.

"So, what are we drinking to? You becoming my brother-in-law?"

"Yes, we can drink to that, if you like." Jake smiled. "Of course, that's assuming the wedding actually goes ahead." He took a sip from his glass, watching Ted over the rim.

"What do you mean, if it goes ahead? What are you talking about?"

"Well, let's see, I'm not sure my sister is going to be quite so willing to marry you once she finds out about your little trips to Duke." He smiled slyly and Ted put his glass down hard, beer spilling over the sides.

"What the hell are you talking about?"

Jake just smiled. Slipping his phone from his pocket, he selected one of the best pictures and slid his phone across the table. Picking it up, Ted looked at the image and felt all the blood drain from his face. Dragging his eyes away from the phone he looked up at Jake, who now had a smug look on his face.

"It's just a bit of fun before I get married. Come on man, you know how it is." He tried to make light of it but he could see that Jake wasn't buying it.

"To you it might be a bit of fun but I doubt my sister, or my folks, will see it that way."

Ted tried to take a deep breath. He felt as if he was going to be sick. He could see everything he had planned, everything he had worked for, disappear in a puff of smoke. *But if he wanted to split them up he would have told her by now, wouldn't he?* It dawned on him then that this wasn't about Jamie. He wanted something. "What do you want from me?"

"What do most blackmailers want? Money." His smug grin wrenched Ted's stomach. He looked so pleased with himself.

"Money? This is about money?" Ted was stunned. This blackmailing little shit came from one of, if not the, wealthiest families around and he wanted *money*?

"You're joking, right?" The shock was clear on his face. "What on earth do you need money for?"

Jake's face darkened. "I wouldn't if you hadn't just stolen my job."

"What on earth are you talking about?"

"Your nice, new job was supposed to be mine. Instead, I got fired. I think it's only fair that you pay my salary from now on since it's your fault."

"So this is all about a spat between you and your dad? Why drag me into it? You're only going to end up hurting your sister!"

Jake slammed his palm on the table, smiling as Ted jumped. "There's only one person here hurting my sister and I'm looking at him. Now, do we have a deal or not?"

"What kind of money are we talking about here?"

"Ten thousand a month. Every month."

His stomach sank. *No way could he find that kind of money!*

"I can't do it, Jake. I don't have that kind of money." It was the wrong thing to say and he watched as a black cloud seemed to cross Jake's face and he sneered.

"Don't give me that, you prick. Your family is loaded. You can easily afford that."

Ted didn't know what to do. If he didn't find the money he had no doubt that Jake would share the photos, and if he explained why he couldn't find the money, then he was sure that he would revel in being able to share that, too. Either way, he was screwed because there was no way that Jamie's parents would let her marry a cheater or a pauper. He needed to buy some time.

"Okay. You're right. But before I pay you a dime, what guarantee do I have that you won't show Jamie the pictures anyway?"

Jake laughed. "There are no guarantees. But if I showed them to her, what motivation would you have to keep paying?"

He had a point. "Okay. Meet me back here tomorrow night and I'll have the cash."

Jake stood up. "Nice doing business with you. Oh, and thanks for the beer."

Ted watched him leave then drained his glass, his hand shaking as he raised it to his lips. What was he going to do?

Seven

He'd had to scrape together every bit of cash he could find, emptying his accounts in the process. It wasn't as if he could go to his folks and ask for the money. They didn't have it in any case.

He couldn't believe he was in this position. He didn't even want to marry Jamie, but he refused to let his family's troubles get out, and they would if they didn't do something soon.

Pulling into the lot outside the bar, he saw that Jake's car was already there. Parking his Porsche next to it, he saw that Jake was sitting inside, waiting for him. Getting out, he walked around to the passenger side and slid in next to him.

"You got the money?"

Ted nodded. "Yes," he replied, taking out an envelope from his jacket pocket and showing him. "It's all here. Ten thousand dollars, as agreed."

Jake reached for it.

"Not so fast." Ted put the envelope back in his pocket, out of Jake's reach. "I can't afford to do this every month. This is a one time deal. Take it or leave it."

Jake's jaw clenched and his eyes turned to steel. "No. That's not what we agreed. 10k every month or my sister sees the photos."

"It's not up for negotiation." Ted's insides felt as if someone was stirring them with a stick. He had to bluff this out. There was no more money, and if Jake didn't back down, he was finished.

Taking the money out of his pocket again, he handed it to him. "This is it. Done. Don't bother me again." Opening the door, he got out of the car. He was sweating and his skin felt clammy. Determined not to look back, to look weak, he strode to his car.

The hand on his shoulder, spinning him around, came as a surprise. He hadn't heard Jake come up behind him. Losing his footing, he fell back, leaning on his car for support.

"Don't you dare walk away from me!" Jake screamed in his face, spittle flying from his mouth. His red face and bulging eyes were inches away. "I *own* you, you piece of shit!"

"Why are you doing this? She's your sister! Why would you want to hurt her?" Ted tried to reason with him.

"*Me* hurt her? You're the one screwing around!" The veins in Jake's neck looked as if they would burst, and Ted tried to back away, almost sliding up on the hood of his car.

Ted could see his plan wasn't working. If anything, Jake seemed to be getting even more out of control.

"*You* get my damn job and *I* get fired! Seem fair to you?" He was breathing really heavily now.

Ted raised his hands in surrender. "Look, I'll turn the job down if it'll make you happy. I don't want to get between you and your dad."

"Just pay the damned money," Jake hissed.

"I can't!"

Ted saw in Jake's eyes the moment he lost it, and everything that came after appeared to happen in slow motion. He watched as Jake pulled his arm back, fist clenched, and swung a punch at his face. Even though he could see it happen, he wasn't able to avoid it and he felt the bones in his cheek crack as Jake's fist made contact. The force of the blow knocked him off his feet and he fell like a dead weight to the ground, hitting his head on a rock as he did.

In the last few seconds before the life left him, his thoughts went to his parents. *Who would help them now?* After that, there was nothing.

***

Shit! What had he done? For a moment, Jake stood stock still as he came out of the fury that had overtaken him. His mind flashed over the last few minutes, and he remembered feeling completely enraged and out of control. Now, as the fog lifted, he saw Ted's body on the ground, bile rising in his throat as panic swept over him.

Quickly glancing around, he checked the parking lot to see if anyone had witnessed what had just happened. *All clear.* Crouching down, he checked for a pulse. Nothing. *Crap!* He'd never meant to lose his temper like that, let alone punch him.

He couldn't stay here. He needed to get far away, and fast. Going back to his own car, he quickly got in and drove out of the lot. Hands sweating on the steering wheel, he quickly turned things over in his head. *Was there anything that would tie him to this?*

The only thing he could think of was the bartender seeing them together the night before. *Think!* He needed an alibi. Just in case. The only person he could think of that would give him one without question was Carrie.

***

Carrie lived in town in an apartment above the hardware store. Parking around the back, he climbed the outside staircase that led to her front door. Banging on it, he waited. *Come on! Be home!* He was relieved when she opened the door.

"Jake. What are you doing here?"

"We need to talk." He walked past her into the apartment.

Looking confused, she closed the door and followed him. "What's wrong?"

Dropping down onto the threadbare couch, Jake dropped his head into his hands. "I screwed up."

She had known about the photos but not what he had planned to do with them, so he told her now. When he got to the part about what had happened that night, she gasped and raised her hands to her mouth.

"Oh, my God! What have you done?" She looked stunned. "Are you sure he was dead?"

"Yeah, I'm sure," he snapped.

Turning to where she'd sat down next to him, he took her hands in his. "I need you to cover for me."

She looked unsure. "What?"

"If the police come asking questions, I need you to cover for me. There's nothing to link me to this so I'm sure they won't." He needed her to agree to this.

"I don't know, Jake. That's a lot to ask of me." She chewed on her bottom lip, not looking him in the eye.

"I know it is, darling, but you know I love you and wouldn't ask if I didn't know you love me, too." He knew exactly what buttons to push and he had to use it to his advantage now. She'd never refused him anything before.

"You truly love me?" she asked him, wide eyes pleading.

"You know I do. I wouldn't want to be with anyone else," he lied glibly.

"Okay. I'll do it."

Jake felt a rush of relief. *Thank God.*

"On one condition."

The relief vanished. *What did she want?* "What?"

"When this all dies down, you tell your parents you want to be with me, that you want to marry me."

Not in this lifetime! That was never going to happen. She was great in the sack and a bit of fun but marry her? No, when he married it would be someone from the right background, not this common piece of trash. "Of course, darling. Absolutely." He was prepared to agree to anything at this point, as long as it got him out of this mess.

"Promise?"

"You have my word."

Seeming satisfied with his answer, she smiled. "Okay. So what happens now?"

"I don't know, I really don't." He shook his head. "I guess someone will find him and call the police and then all hell breaks loose."

It didn't seem real. A few days ago the only thing he'd had to worry about was getting a promotion. Now he was a murderer.

***

He'd been lying there all night, just staring at the ceiling. Though it was the last thing he'd wanted to do, he'd had no choice but to spend the night at Carrie's place. All he'd really wanted was to go home and be alone, to try and absorb what had happened.

Turning his head slightly, he watched Carrie as she slept, on her side with her back to him. He could hear her slow and steady breathing in the silence of the room.

She had really surprised him tonight, and not in a good way. He'd expected her to be much more upset than she had been. He'd just told her he'd killed a man, but she'd taken it in her stride. There had been no disgust, no anger, not even any compassion for Ted or his sister.

He hadn't been able to stop thinking about it, staring blankly at the television screen while they watched a movie. He had hardly spoken at all, just waiting for the police to arrive and drag him away.

When they'd decided to go to bed and she'd wanted sex, he'd had to physically push her off him. Had she really thought he'd feel like it after what he'd just done?

As he watched her chest rise and fall now, he realized that, actually, he hardly knew anything about this woman. He hadn't wanted to, but maybe he should make it his business to find out. He had a feeling there was a lot more to her than met the eye.

Eight

The pounding on her bedroom door woke her. Fighting off sleep, she reached for the clock on her bedside table. Who on earth was making that racket at 2 a.m.?

"Hang on, I'm coming!" she shouted, as she slipped out of bed and grabbed her robe. Putting it on, she opened her bedroom door.

"What's going on, Mom?" she asked when she saw her mother standing there. "Are you okay?"

"Oh, Jamie! It's awful!" It was obvious she'd been crying as she took her by the hand and led her back into her room, sitting down on the bed and pulling her down next to her.

"Mom, I'm getting worried. What's happened?" She had a horrible feeling in the pit of her stomach now.

"I'm so sorry, Jamie. It's Ted. He's dead."

Shocked, she just looked at her mom for a moment. "What on earth are you talking about?"

"He was found tonight in the parking lot of a bar outside town. It looks like he was in a fight. I'm so sorry, darling." Tears rolled down her cheeks as she reached for a tissue.

No. This was insane. There had to be some mistake. Pulling her hand out of her mother's, she stood up.

"No you're wrong. I'll just call him and we'll clear this up." She walked over to her dresser and picked up her phone.

Her mom followed her and gently took the phone from her hand. "Jamie, there's no mistake. I'm so sorry."

It hit her then, all of it. Her knees gave way and she crumpled. Her father, who'd been standing in the doorway, reached her just before she hit the floor.

***

As light filtered through her eyelids, Jamie remembered. *No!* Her eyes flew open and as they focused, she saw her mom sitting in the chair beside her bed, watching her intently. She'd obviously been sitting there all night without sleeping. Her eyes were puffy and she had dark circles under her eyes.

"You're awake!" She got to her feet and came to sit on the bed.

"What happened?" She felt groggy and her head felt as if had been stuffed full of cotton.

"You fainted, darling. When you came around you were hysterical, so we had the doctor come by and give you something to help you sleep."

That explained the fuzziness. "It's true, then?" she whispered.

Her mother nodded. "I'm so sorry."

"What happened? Do they know yet? Who found him?" She had so many questions.

"The police don't know, yet. Someone leaving the bar found him on the ground next to his car. They want to talk to you, darling."

"Who does?"

"The police," she said gently.

Jamie nodded. Of course they did, and she wanted to talk to them, too. "Okay, give me five minutes to get dressed."

She pushed the covers back and swung her legs around to get out of bed. A wave of dizziness stopped her and, putting her hands on her knees, she lowered her head and breathed deeply.

Her mom looked horrified. "You're not speaking to them now! They can wait until you're feeling a bit stronger."

"No. I want to talk to them." She knew that it hadn't sunk in yet and that when it did, it would destroy her and she wouldn't be able to function. She wanted to talk to them before that happened.

"No, darling, I simply won't allow it!"

"Mom, please. Let me do this." Her sigh told her that she knew there was no point arguing with her.

"Okay, but I'll be there with you. There's an officer downstairs who's been here waiting for you to wake up. I'll go and tell him you'll be down when you're dressed." She stood up. "Will you be okay on your own for a few minutes?"

"I'll be fine," she assured her. "I'll be down in a few minutes."

She didn't move until her mother had left the room and closed the door softly behind her.

The pain came then. In great crashing waves, it washed over her, leaving her gasping for breath. She couldn't do anything but grip her sheets tightly in her fists, sucking in air as if she were drowning. She could feel the tears stream down her cheeks and drop off her chin, but she didn't try to stop them. Couldn't have if she'd wanted to.

She stayed like that for a few minutes, until she felt the waves start to recede and she was able to catch her breath again. Gradually, her head started to clear and she was able to get control of her grief. At least for now.

Standing up on wobbly legs, she went to the bathroom and washed her face, allowing the cool water to wash away the tears and sooth the puffiness around her eyes. The sight of herself in the mirror startled her. To anyone else she would look exactly the same, but she could see it. She had been dealt a cruel blow and it showed in her eyes. Part of her had died.

Taking a long, deep breath, she made a promise. *When I find out who did this to you, I will make them pay.*

Calmer now, she got dressed and went downstairs to speak to the police.

Nine

His eyes felt gritty as he tried to concentrate on the road ahead, that grittiness you get when you haven't slept. He hadn't been able to go back to sleep so he'd just laid there as the darkness turned from inky black to cobalt blue, signaling the arrival of dawn.

What he had done bothered him, but he would deal with it. What was bothering him more was the thought of losing everything if he got caught. As soon as the sun had appeared over the horizon, he'd gotten out of bed, dressed, and headed home.

Turning off the main road onto the driveway, he wondered what he would find. They would have found Ted's body by now, no doubt. The police cruiser parked outside the house confirmed his thoughts and he took a deep breath to settle his nerves before getting out of the car and going indoors. *Showtime.*

"What's going on?" he asked studiously, keeping his face blank.

"Ah, Jake." His father stood up from where he'd been on the couch in the living room. "This is Officer Casey." He gestured to the uniformed officer standing next to him. "Something terrible has happened, I'm afraid." He took a deep breath. "Ted has been killed."

Jake pretended to be shocked. He needed this to look genuine.

"Oh, my God! What happened?" He listened to the details as if he didn't already know them, making appropriately horrified comments, desperately wanting to ask if the police had any leads.

"Where's Jamie? Is she okay?" He felt a twinge of guilt as he thought of what this must be doing to his sister, but it didn't last long. It was about survival now.

"She's upstairs with your mother. She's just been talking to the officer here and it was quite upsetting. I would leave them alone for now, son." His dad placed a hand on his shoulder and gave it a squeeze. "She's going to need our support."

Jake nodded, placing his own hand on top of his father's. "Of course."

"So, what do you know?" He addressed the question to the police officer.

"Not a lot yet, I'm afraid," the officer said, shaking his head. "The bar doesn't have any surveillance cameras and no one saw what happened. We're still trying to trace a couple of the regulars who were in earlier, but so far, I'm afraid, we have nothing."

"Had he been robbed?"

"No, it doesn't look like a robbery. His wallet and car were still there and the keys were in the ignition. If robbery had been the motive, I'm sure they wouldn't have passed up an opportunity like that."

Jake quietly let out a breath. *They were clueless!*

"So, what happens now?"

"Well, we've spoken to Miss McKay and your parents, so now we just need to speak to you when you're over the shock. We can't afford to wait too long, though."

"No need to wait for me. You can talk to me now. Anything I can do to help, I will."

"I'll leave you to it, Jake. I'm going to check on your sister," his father said with a nod to the police officer. "Anything you need, you call me, understood?" Without waiting for a reply, he turned and left the room.

"Thank you for your cooperation. This won't take long." The officer gestured to the couch. "Shall we sit down?"

Jake sat, somehow managing to keep his expression blank.

"Now, I apologize, but I have to ask this. Where were you last night after 9 p.m.?"

"Is that when they think he was killed?"

"We haven't had the time of death from the medical examiner yet, but a customer recalls leaving the bar at that time and the lot was empty then."

"Ah, okay." Jake made a show of thinking about where he was. "I was at my girlfriend's house. Carrie Taylor. I was there from about 7 p.m. on."

The officer made a note. "And what time did you leave?"

Jake smiled conspiratorially. "About half an hour ago."

The officer responded with a brief smile. "We're going to need to speak to her. Just routine, you understand."

"Of course."

"Thank you, that's all I need for now. If there is anything else the detectives will be in touch."

Shaking his hand, Jake walked him to the door and watched as he got into his squad car and drove off. He waited until he was sure he was gone then slid his phone from his pocket, realizing that his hands were shaking. Stepping outside so that he couldn't be overheard, he dialed Carrie's number.

He spoke as soon as she answered. "The police were here when I got home. I told them I was at your place all night from early evening, as agreed."

"Did they suspect anything?"

"I don't think so, but they said they'd have to speak to you, which we knew was going to happen. You know what you need to say, right?"

She sighed. "Of course. I'm not an idiot."

He let out a breath. "I know. Sorry. Just a bit stressed over here."

"Don't worry about it. It'll be fine. They've got nothing on you. I'll call you when they're gone."

Disconnecting, Jake turned to look at the house. All this was going to be his one day and nothing, *nothing*, was going to get in the way of that.

Ten

It had been three weeks since the murder, three of the longest weeks of her life. Every morning, just for a brief instant in time, she forgot. In that instant, she was happy. But it was all too fleeting and when reality quickly dawned on her, her happiness was once again shattered.

She'd gotten into a routine now. She'd get up, have breakfast, and then be right on the phone to the police to see if there was any news. For the first few days she'd been hopeful, never doubting that someone would be caught and that she'd be able to see them pay for what they'd done. As the days passed and there was no progress, no miraculous, scientific breakthrough like you see in the movies, her fear grew. Fear that whoever did this was going to be able to stay free.

There was no denying that as her hopes faded, her anger grew. Surprisingly, it wasn't aimed at the killer but rather was aimed at herself. All those stupid doubts she'd had, her anger at Ted for wanting a quick wedding, all seemed so silly now. She'd marry him tomorrow and never worry about the little things again if she could just have him back.

Her family had been incredibly supportive, especially Jake. Those first few days, he'd just sat at the bottom of her bed not saying a word, just keeping her company. He'd gone with her to see the police when she'd wanted to, regardless of whether they had any news or not. Physically going to the station, talking to the officers, helped her feel like she was doing something. He'd sat with her when she'd gone to see Ted's parents to discuss the funeral arrangements, holding her hand quietly.

And he was by her side now as they followed the coffin to the cemetery for the burial. There was no doubt in her mind that this was going to be one of the hardest days of her life, but she knew that with her brother's help, she'd get through it.

***

It was almost over. He'd hardly left Jamie's side since the murder. He liked to think he was just being a good brother but he knew he was kidding himself. He wanted to be close in case the police came up with anything. He needed to know the moment they did.

So far, though, they had nothing, and with no further avenues of investigation open to them, they'd finally released Ted's body for burial.

Looking around, he frowned when he saw Carrie standing there, her head bowed, at the back of the circle of mourners surrounding the grave. As he watched, she raised her head and met his eyes, smiling. She'd insisted on coming to the wake, but he'd told her to meet him at the house. He'd had no idea she'd turn up here.

The priest had just finished and the mourners started dispersing, making their way to their vehicles to drive over to Ted parent's house.

"Go and get in the car. I'll be there in just a second." He kissed his sister's cheek and watched as she walked off in the direction of the black limousine parked a short distance away.

Everyone had left the graveside now except Carrie, who was waiting for him.

"What are you doing here? I told you I'd meet you at the house."

"I wanted to pay my respects. It's a free country, you know."

"Pay your respects? But you didn't even know him!"

"Actually, I did." She looked at him and sighed. "We had a bit of a 'thing' a few months ago."

She said this so casually that for a moment, Jake was lost for words. "I'm sorry? A 'thing'?"

She nodded. "Yeah. Don't worry, it was before I met you."

He couldn't believe she was telling him this, here, now.

"And you think now is the right time to be telling me this?" He could feel his face getting flushed. "You don't think maybe you should have told me this before?"

She looked genuinely confused. "Why? It doesn't have anything to do with you. I'm only telling you now so you know why I needed to come."

Jake shook his head, bewildered. She was right; it had nothing to do with him really, other than the fact that it was further evidence that Ted was a serial cheater. It certainly didn't bother him.

"For God's sake, just make sure Jamie doesn't find out. She'll run straight to my parents and, let's face it, they already have a pretty low opinion of you," he snapped.

"Give me some credit will you!"

"I'll see you up at the house." He glared at her as he turned to walk away.

"Wait! Can I go with you? I took a taxi here. I didn't bring the car in case I wanted to drink."

"No, you can't come with us. We're in the funeral car. It's not appropriate. You'll have to get a ride from someone or get another cab."

Leaving her standing there pouting, he headed to the car where Jamie was waiting.

Eleven

"I told you, not yet," Jake hissed.

"When, then?"

They were having the same old disagreement again. She'd been pushing him to tell his parents about their plans for the past week. Every time they were alone together, she'd bring the subject up.

"Jeez, Carrie! We're at a wake. Will you just quit?" He was getting seriously pissed now.

He wouldn't have a choice. He knew that. He'd have to tell them at some point. If he didn't follow through on his promise, then he had no doubt whatsoever that she would go straight to Jamie and his parents and he would lose everything.

He was struggling with the guilt. Every time he saw Jamie's ravaged, tear-streaked face he felt sick to his stomach. He had done this to her, he had caused her this pain. It may have been unintentional, but the result was the same. There was nothing he could do to change things, but he was determined that he would do everything he could to make her smile again.

"Okay, okay! We'll give it a couple of days and then we tell them. Agreed?"

With a sigh, he nodded. "Agreed."

That seemed to put a smile on her face and she wandered off happily to pick at the buffet.

***

She was feeling quite pleased with herself. That ring was practically on her finger. She could almost feel it!

She wasn't naïve. She knew how most of the men she had relationships with saw her: the cheap whore worth a lay but not worth anything else. She probably hadn't helped herself by screwing half the men in town and getting herself a reputation for being easy. But she was determined to marry into money, to escape her life.

Her mom had raised her, if it could be called that, in a trailer singlehandedly, and she had no idea who her father was. He could have been any one of the trail of men that traipsed through her mother's life, leaving nothing but bruises and heartache.

At the first chance she'd gotten she'd left, taking her mother's current beau with her. She'd been sixteen and he'd been forty-four but he had his own car and a job and that was enough for her. She'd stuck with him for about six months, until she'd grown tired of his old body on top of hers. Then she'd relieved him of his cash and hit the road.

She'd ended up here and somehow she'd stayed. Ted had been her first chance at marrying well but it hadn't gone according to plan. Then Jake had come along. She'd done everything she could to make sure that she was the perfect woman. She hadn't been demanding, had played it cool, and had screwed him senseless whenever he wanted her to.

When he'd come to her that night wanting an alibi, she'd known that was it. Home run.

And now, the end was in sight. Soon she would have that damned ring on her finger and people would stop looking down their noses at her. She might even go back and find her mother and buy her a new trailer. She laughed out loud at that thought, drawing glances from the other mourners. *Jeez, relax people!*

Filling her plate with food, she looked around the room as she ate. God, there was so much money in this room! And soon, she would be one of them. She only just managed to suppress her grin at this thought. She could see the sideways glances now from people wondering what on earth she was doing here. More than a couple, she knew, were wondering if their wives or girlfriends were going to get a nasty shock.

Spotting Jamie standing alone by one of the room's many windows looking lost, she made her way over to her.

"How you doing? You okay?"

Jamie looked confused for moment, her eyes unfocused.

"Sorry, I was miles away." She smiled weakly. "I'm okay. Thank you for asking. I was just thinking about how unfair it is that such a good man should die so young."

"Um. Yeah." *If she only knew what kind of a man he really was!* "So they still don't know anything, huh?" She knew the answer, but she had to ask.

"No, nothing." Tears rolled down her cheeks as she wrung her hands. "Our whole future, snatched away, and I still don't know why!"

"What did you say to her?" The question made her jump. She hadn't heard Jake approach. "Has she upset you?" He put his arm around his sister, pulling her slightly away from Carrie.

Of course it had to be her fault! "No, I didn't!"

He just glared at her.

"She was being really nice, actually." Jamie sniffed, dabbing at her eyes with a tissue. "Saying what a nice man Ted was."

I was?

"Well, that surprises me, actually. I didn't think you and Ted got along that well." He looked at her quizzically. "When I saw you at the party, it looked like the two of you had been fighting, remember?"

"Why were you fighting?" Jamie was looking at her also now and she felt like a rabbit caught in headlights.

"Really, it was nothing." She tried to pass it off. "Look, I'd better go. I've got to work later and I need to go home and get ready. Will you drop me off?" she asked Jake.

"I don't really want to leave Jamie. Can you make your own way back?"

"I didn't drive, you know that," she hissed back. *She's in a room full of people fawning over her. She'll be fine,* is what she actually wanted to say but that would be rude.

"No, go. Take her home. I'll be fine." Jamie smiled at him.

"You sure?"

"I'm sure. Go."

Twelve

He was not looking forward to this at all. It had only been a week since the funeral, but Carrie was getting increasingly upset and he knew that if he didn't speak to his parents soon she was likely to shoot her mouth off. He'd told them he had something important to talk to them about and they were both now standing in the living room of the house waiting for them.

"Seriously, Carrie, do you have to be here? Why can't I talk to them by myself?" He just knew that it was going to make it so much harder with her present.

"Because I know what you're like, and I want to make sure that you don't back down."

"I won't. I just think it would be better coming from me. On my own."

"Better coming from you? Jeez! You sound like you're going to give them bad news! You're telling them you're getting married. Any normal parents would be happy for you."

"It's not as simple as that and you know it." *She knew how his parents felt about her, why did she have to make it so much more difficult?*

Before she could answer, the door opened and his father walked in with his mother just behind. She pulled up short when she saw Carrie.

"What is she doing here?"

"This involves her, Mom."

"Well, get on with it then. We haven't got all day, you know," his father barked at him.

Jake cleared his throat, trying to think of the best way to put it. However he said it, he knew that it wouldn't be well received. Carrie was looking at him with an exasperated expression on her face.

"For God's sake, will you just tell them?"

"Okay, okay." *Oh well, here goes.* "I've asked Carrie to marry me."

The silence that followed was so long he thought that maybe he hadn't actually spoken out loud. He was just about to repeat himself when his mother spoke.

"I really hope this is some kind of sick joke."

He shook his head. "No, it's true. We're getting married."

His father still hadn't said a word.

"Dad?"

"Is she pregnant?" he asked him, not even looking at Carrie.

Carrie threaded her arm through his. "No, I'm not pregnant."

"If she's not pregnant, what's the rush, for God's sake?" his mom snapped. "Can't you at least wait until Jamie's had a few months to grieve before you hit her with this?"

***

She'd had enough of this. It was about time someone told Jake's parents how it was going to be and it clearly wasn't going to be him. "Why should we wait? Ted's dead and buried."

Jake parents looked at her with distaste. "Jake, I think you should take some time. Make sure this is the right thing to do," his mom said desperately. "And I know you don't want to hurt your sister. Hearing news like this right now will be devastating for her."

That was the last straw. "For God's sake! He was only marrying her for her money, anyway. It wasn't the love of the century or anything!" She couldn't help herself. "Probably did her a favor, him getting himself killed!"

They all turned then at the sound of a loud gasp coming from the doorway. Jamie stood there with her hands raised to her mouth, her eyes wide in shock.

"How dare you say such a thing! It's not true!" she screamed at Carrie, hands now clenched into fists at her side.

"It is true," Carrie sneered. "His whole family is broke. You were going to be the golden goose that got them out of the mess they're in."

Jamie launched herself across the room at her then, hands grabbing for her hair and face. Reacting quickly, Jake grabbed Jamie by the waist and held her, arms and legs flailing, preventing her from reaching her target.

"Calm down, she didn't mean it," he said to her, trying to keep her under control, glaring across the room at Carrie.

"Take your fiancée and get her out of here. Now," barked his father. Gingerly letting go of Jamie, pausing to make sure she wasn't about to fly at Carrie again, she felt Jake take her by the arm and pull her out of the room.

"What the hell do you think you were doing in there?" he hissed at her as he pulled her out the front door and to the car.

"Shit. Sorry. They just got under my skin, treating me like I'm dirt and going on about Saint Jamie." She slammed the passenger door shut, turning to him. "It's not fair. They can't even be happy for us."

Jake didn't say a word as he started the car and one look at his thunderous expression told her she should just let it go. So she would. For now.

Thirteen

She was struggling to hold the tears back as she drove. *It couldn't be true could it?* She had to find out. She couldn't go and ask Ted's parents. They were grieving, too. It would be unforgivable to go storming in there asking intensely private questions, especially if everything Carrie had said was a lie. No, she had to go back to the horse's mouth and see Carrie, but this time alone.

She'd had to wait all day until Jake had come home, wanting to make sure he was out of the way before she left, and then she'd had to sneak out without being seen. These days, her parents hardly let her out of their sight and they would undoubtedly question where she was going if they saw her leave.

Pulling up and parking out back, Jamie checked her face in the mirror in her car. The tears had dried, leaving her face blotchy and her eyes puffy. *At least I'm not crying any more,* she thought to herself as she climbed the stairs and knocked on Carrie's apartment door. She'd already checked at the diner and been told that today was her day off, so she was hoping to catch her at home.

She was rewarded by the sound of locks turning and the door being opened.

"Oh. It's you."

"Can I come in?" Judging from her face, Jamie was clearly the last person she'd been expecting to knock at her door.

"I suppose so," she replied, pulling the door open wider so that Jamie could come inside. "To what do I owe the pleasure of this visit? Or do I even need to ask?" she said, sitting down on the couch.

"May I?" Jamie asked. She didn't really want to sit but her legs were a bit wobbly and she didn't want to collapse in a heap in front of this woman.

Carrie nodded. "So?"

Jamie took a deep breath. "I want you to tell me more about what you said yesterday. I need to know if it's true."

"It's true, all right. Why would I lie?"

"To hurt me, though God knows what I've ever done to you."

"Here we go again. It's always got to be all about you, doesn't it? Princess Jamie," Carrie snarled. "Well, guess what? This time, it's not all about you. It's about me and Jake, *our* future, and I'm sick of everything being on hold because of you."

Jamie was taken aback at the hostility coming from her. "I have no idea what you're talking about!"

"You really don't see it, do you? First Ted, and now Jake. You always have to come first."

"Ted? Of course I came first with Ted. Why on earth would that affect you?" Jamie looked at her quizzically.

"Because even when I was sleeping with him, I had to hear about you all the goddamn time. About how important his damn wedding to you was for his whole family."

The room started to go out of focus then and she felt the black hole that had been threatening her since Ted had been killed engulf her.

"What do you mean, when you were sleeping with him?" She had no idea how she'd managed to speak, let alone keep her voice so calm.

Carrie looked at her as if she were stupid. "Like I told you already, he was marrying you because he had to, but he wasn't about to go without, was he? We had a lot of fun, him and I. He was a great lay"

She didn't know how, but somehow she made it to Carrie's bathroom just in time, throwing up in the toilet until she was empty. Shaking, she stayed on the floor, leaning her back against the bathroom wall. *What on earth did Jake see in this woman?* She'd come here for answers and she'd gotten a lot more than she bargained for.

Once she was sure she wasn't going to throw up again, she pushed herself to her feet. *I need to get out of here.* Throwing open the bathroom door, she pushed past Carrie, who was standing just outside and, on unsteady legs, left the apartment, slamming the door behind her.

***

Hell! She stood for a moment watching the door after she'd gone, as if expecting her to suddenly come back but it remained firmly closed.

Dammit! What had she done! Grabbing her cell from the kitchen counter, she quickly dialed Jake's number.

Come on! Pick up! she urged, as it rang and rang. Finally, just as she was about to put it down and try again, he answered.

"Jamie's been here," she said before he had a chance to say anything.

"What? What for?" Jake said, sounding shaken.

"Well, I didn't invite her!" she shouted. "She wanted to know about Ted, about what I said yesterday."

"What did you tell her?"

"The same as I told her yesterday, the truth. That he wanted her for her money."

"You stupid bitch! That's all we damn well need. It's bad enough I have to marry you without getting my parents pissed." She could hear him take a deep breath. "My father is not beyond cutting me out of his will completely if I marry you. He's gonna take a lot of convincing not to as it is, and I doubt that's what you want, is it?"

Of course it wasn't. The whole point of going through with this was so that she could be rich. There wouldn't be much point if he got cut off.

"Of course it's not. You've got to stop her. She's on her way to see your parents."

"How much does she know? Does she know about me?" The panic was oozing into his every word.

"No, just Ted. Everything about Ted."

"Please tell me she doesn't know about you two?"

"I'm sorry. It just slipped out!"

Everything was going wrong. She could see her bright, rich future slipping away.

"We've got to stop her before she gets home. Talk to her, try and get her to see sense."

"Right. You stay where you are and I'll go and meet her. She'll listen to me." The silence in her ear told her that he'd put the phone down without waiting for a reply.

She couldn't just sit here and wait. That precious princess was not going to ruin the best chance she'd ever had at having a decent future. She could catch up with them and maybe help Jake talk some sense into her. Grabbing her keys from the kitchen counter, she ran out the door.

***

His thoughts were falling over themselves as he raced down the driveway. It was all getting horribly out of hand. He'd never meant to hurt Ted. It wasn't like he was a killer. All he'd ever wanted was to be treated the same as Jamie. If his asshole of a father hadn't fired him, none of this would have happened. Now he was stuck, engaged to a woman he didn't want to marry but would because she could get him locked away for life and with a sister running around like a loose cannon, very possibly about to ruin everything.

His whole life was unravelling before his eyes. If he could just get to Jamie, stop her from coming between him and Carrie, then the secret would stay buried. It would all pass with time and no one would be any the wiser.

He couldn't be cut off. He'd earned a big payday after putting up with all the years of crap his dad had dished out. He *wouldn't* end up with nothing. He couldn't let that happen.

Pushing his foot down harder on the gas pedal, he raced to head off Jamie on her way back from town.

Fourteen

Did she even know him? The tears streamed down her face, blurring her vision, as she tried to keep the car on the road. *Was all her pain based on lies?*

No, it couldn't be true. Carrie was obviously just a woman with an axe to grind and she was her chosen target, though she had no idea why. One thing she did know; there was no way she could let her brother marry that evil woman. She would tear their family apart.

Her tears were slowing now, their tracks cooling on her skin and, gradually, her breathing was returning to normal. She refused to believe the lies that woman told. One thing was for sure, though. She was going to make it her mission to get her out of their lives.

She'd gotten about halfway home when her car suddenly started making sputtering sounds. Looking down at the dash, she realized she was out of gas. In all the excitement, she'd forgotten to fill up and it was now drawing the last drops from the bottom of her tank.

Dammit! Pulling over to the side of the road, she got out of the car and slammed the door shut. She was several miles from home still and, looking around, miles from anywhere else, it seemed. All around her were empty fields and nothing else. Looking up and down the road, she saw nothing but emptiness.

Checking her pockets, she realized with a sinking feeling that she didn't have her cell phone. She'd left it charging in her room back at the house. *Could this day get any worse!* Realizing there was nothing she could do except wait, she sat on the trunk of her car so she could flag down anyone coming.

She didn't have long to wait, and after a few minutes she saw a car approaching in the distance, a car she recognized. Waiting until it pulled up alongside her, she explained that she was out of fuel and gratefully opened the door and climbed into the passenger seat.

There was no reason to think that she'd just made the biggest mistake of her life. Not yet, anyway.

Fifteen

It was the first raindrop that woke her. It landed on her cheek before sliding sideways toward her ear. It was quickly followed by many more, splashing onto her face and closed eyelids, bringing her back to consciousness.

Bringing a hand to her face to wipe away the dampness, Jamie groaned. *Oh, that hurt!* Rolling onto her side, she opened her eyes and looked around. *What the hell?* The bed of leaves she had been lying on rustled as she brought herself to a sitting position, every part of her body crying out in pain. Looking down at herself, she saw her shirt was torn and covered in her own blood. Pushing herself to her knees, she looked around, panicked. *Where was she?*

The rain was coming down faster now, the drops hitting the trees all around her sounding like the dull roar of a train. Leaning on a nearby tree trunk for support, she eased herself to her feet. Her feet were bare and the debris on the forest floor dug into their soles. Looking down, she saw that her legs were scraped and bloodied, though the blood had dried. Confused, she tentatively checked the rest of herself and saw that the damage wasn't limited to her legs. Her arms and hands were in a similar state and, raising a hand to her face, it felt oddly swollen.

Despite this, it wasn't her injuries that scared her. Or the fact that she seemed to be in the middle of nowhere with no idea where she was. No. What scared her was that she had no idea how she had gotten here or, in fact, any memory at all.

***

She lost track of time as she stumbled through the forest. The rain had soaked her clothing and it clung to her skin as she walked, her feet bleeding now, trying to find a road, a house, anything. She'd reached the point of exhaustion, close to giving up, when she felt a change in the surface below her feet. She was so tired she'd been walking with her eyes almost closed and hadn't noticed the trees thinning until the only thing before her was road. Falling to her knees, she didn't even have the strength to cry and she welcomed the darkness that came then.

Sixteen

A year-and-a-half later

Her feet were killing her again, the pain shooting all the way up to her knees like hundreds of hot little darts. Cursing, she stopped and leaned against a nearby lamppost. There was no way she was going to hobble all the way back to her apartment like this. Barefoot it was, then.

Reaching down, she unzipped first her left, then her right boot, slipping her feet out and onto the cool pavement. *God, that felt so good!* Picking up the boots, she walked on keeping her eyes firmly on the ground in front of her. This was not the best part of town and the last thing she needed was to step on some user's discarded needle.

Belle loved this time of the day, that time just between night and day, when the sky was lightening but the sun had yet to show itself over the horizon. The roads were quiet, the late night revellers fast asleep and the early risers only just waking up and it felt as if she had the world to herself. Sometimes she played a little game with herself and imagined she was somewhere else entirely. Walking along the banks of the Seine in

Paris, or floating down the Nile in Egypt. Anywhere but here.

Turning the last corner, she arrived at the door that led to her apartment. Calling it an apartment probably made it sound grander than it was. It was really no more than two rooms above the laundromat. It consisted of only two filthy, dank rooms with a roach problem. She tried to keep it nice, she'd made some pretty curtains for the windows and some cushions for the couch, but there was no denying it was a dump. It was all that she could afford, though, so she made the best of it and she was determined that it wouldn't be forever.

At least she had her own roof over her head. It was more than she'd had when she had first gotten into town. Exhausted, she climbed the stairs and let herself in, thankful that the night was over.

"You're finally back, then?"

The sound of the voice made her jump almost out of her skin. "What are you doing here?" She hated it when he let himself in.

"It's payday. I've been waiting here for an hour, and you know how much I don't like being kept waiting."

It was hard to believe that she'd once thought this man was her salvation, her knight in shining armor. Looking at him now, all she saw was a creep. In his late twenties, Blade looked much older. He'd grown up on the street and every fight, every abuse, showed on his face. It was a hard face, aged before its time, and the crooked nose and scar running from his right ear to the corner of his mouth gave him a menacing air. It was strange; that first day when they'd met, when he'd found her at the side of the road, he hadn't looked menacing. In fact, she'd barely noticed the scar at all as he picked her up and helped her into his car.

She knew better now, though. Reaching into her left boot, she lifted the sole and pulled out the bundle of notes that she'd stashed there and handed it to him. She watched in silence as he counted them out.

"Is this it?" he snapped, looking up at her from the threadbare couch where he sat.

"It's not my fault. It was really quiet last night." She tried to hold his gaze as he stared at her, but she couldn't and had to look away. In an instant, he was on his feet and gripped her face in one hand, squeezing hard. She could feel his hot breath on her face as he brought his face close to hers.

"Do you take me for a fool?"

She tried to shake her head but couldn't; his grip on her face was too tight.

"If I find you're keeping a little something back for yourself, I'll kill you. You know that, right?" he hissed in her face.

This time she managed a nod.

"Well, I guess this will have to do, then," he said, letting go of her face and stuffing the bills in the pocket of his pants. "I'll see you in a couple of days and you'd better have more for me next time."

She didn't move until he slammed the apartment door behind him. Rushing to it, she leaned against it until she heard the downstairs door open and then close. Satisfied that he'd gone, she bolted the door and walked over to the couch and sat down, her knees trembling and her heart beating way too fast.

After waiting for a few minutes, just to be sure that he wasn't going to come back again, she took her remaining boot off and pulled out the few bills she'd stashed there. She knew that if he ever checked she'd be dead, but it was a risk she was prepared to take. She'd never be able to get away from him, from this life, if she didn't have a bit of money put aside.

Standing up, she pulled the couch away from the wall and dropped to her knees. Finding what she was looking for, she pried up one of the floorboards with her fingernails. It came away easily in her hand, revealing a small space underneath. Taking the plastic bag that was hidden there, she opened it and took out a bundle of bills, adding today's to the pile. She had about a thousand bucks put aside now. Clutching the bundle to her chest as she knelt there on the floor, she closed her eyes briefly and allowed herself to imagine a different life.

She'd already decided where she would go. Florida. She imagined herself getting a little apartment, a nice clean one where she didn't have to worry about roaches crawling over her as she slept, and a job. Waitressing, probably, as she couldn't do anything else, but as long as it wasn't selling herself she was fine with that. The thought brought a smile to her lips and reinforced her determination. She would get out of here. She just had to.

After putting the money back and moving the couch back into position she took a quick shower, scrubbing every inch of her skin, before pulling the fold-away bed down from the wall and crawling under the covers. She was exhausted.

Sleep eluded her, though, as it usually did. Inevitably, her thoughts turned again to that day when she had met Billy for the first time. He was Billy to her then, before he revealed his true intentions and told her that his street name was Blade and that was what she should call him.

She had been so frightened and confused when he'd found her by the side of the road that day that she had just been grateful to see a friendly face and had accepted his offer of a ride. She'd instantly passed out again on the back seat and when she had woken several hours later, she had been in a warm, comfortable bed and her wounds had been cleaned. For the first couple of days she had remained there, too exhausted to do anything other than recover, but once her strength had started to return she had started asking questions.

What she had discovered had shocked her to the core. Billy had explained that he had been driving back from visiting a friend when he had come across her at the side of the road, three hundred miles from where she now lay, and had instantly recognized her from the TV. He'd explained that she was wanted for the murder of a shop keeper following a robbery gone bad, and that her photo had been all over the local TV news.

Rather than turn her in, he had brought her here and was prepared to look after her. What choice did she have? She couldn't go to the hospital or the police, despite not knowing so much as her own name, or she would have been instantly thrown in jail. So, she'd gradually come to rely on Billy more and more.

It was several weeks later that things changed. She'd been watching TV, waiting for him to come home, when she'd heard his key in the lock, along with another voice she didn't recognize. Taking her to one side, he'd explained that he owed quite a lot of money to this man and could she, just this once, take care of it for him? She'd been confused at first, not realizing immediately what he meant, but then what he was asking of her dawned on her.

She'd refused at first, disgusted that he would even ask, foolishly believing that she had a choice. Her tears hadn't swayed him, though, and it hadn't taken him long to point out that her alternatives were limited.

If she didn't do as he asked, didn't help him out of the situation after all he'd done for her, then why should he keep her secret? Why shouldn't he just go right then and tell the police exactly where she was? She'd broken down then, pleading with him not to make her do it, but he'd just gotten angry and slapped her across the face and told her to do as she was told.

She'd been completely numb as she'd followed the stranger into the bedroom and allowed him on top of her. It hadn't taken long, a matter of minutes, but after that, there had been no going back.

It happened more and more often until it didn't even come as a shock when she realized money was changing hands and she was not helping him pay of his debts as she'd been told.

It had been a short step from there to where she was now, selling her body to line his pockets and trying to hide enough away to make a new start somewhere else.

Exhaustion finally overtook her and sleep came.

Seventeen

Everybody had left and she was finally alone, the only sound the tapping of the raindrops as they hit the leaves on their way to the ground. Kat barely noticed. Looking at the twin mounds of freshly turned earth in front of her, she couldn't believe that her only sister was dead, killed by the drunk driver that had ploughed into her car, killing her brother-in-law, too. It took a huge effort to turn away and look toward the car waiting for her nearby with the lone figure of her nephew waiting for her, holding an umbrella.

Saying a last goodbye, she turned and picked her way across the sodden ground.

"I'm so sorry, Jake." She reached for his hand but he turned away, opening the car door for her before she could touch him. He didn't speak until they were both in the car and out of the rain. He reached for the ignition but then stopped, his hand resting on the keys.

"Why didn't you come? She needed you," he said, not looking at her.

She knew exactly what he meant. Jamie had been missing for eighteen months now. When she'd first received the news, she'd been devastated and had called her sister every day. She'd convinced herself that she didn't need to come because the local police were doing everything they could. She knew that because she was a cop herself.

To reassure herself, she'd made contact with the local chief of police and she'd been satisfied that he knew what he was doing. As time had gone on, with no news, the phone calls had started to wane until they'd dwindled to one every couple of weeks. She'd been so wrapped up in herself, in trying to keep her job after her unauthorized jaunt to the UK with her old partner, Kyle, that she'd told herself that her sister had her husband; she didn't need her getting under her feet.

Looking out of the car window at the graves, she knew that her decision to put her job first would haunt her for the rest of her life.

"I don't know what to say, Jake. I was wrong. I'm here now, though, and I'll stay as long as you need me."

He didn't reply; he merely nodded and started the car.

Eighteen

The day dawned with not a cloud in sight and the bright sunlight on her eyelids woke her. For a blissful moment, a brief millisecond, she forgot why she was here, in her sister's house, but then it all came back to her. She was gone.

They'd never been close, even growing up, but they'd always loved each other. They'd come from a good local family and their parents had had high ambitions for them. Kat had let them down, though, and, after causing a local scandal, had left home at nineteen and had never returned. Even for her parents' funerals.

It felt strange being back, and she almost felt like that frightened kid again. But she was a different person now. She'd gone through a lot after she'd left, but she'd dragged herself up and she was proud of what she'd achieved. It took a lot of hard work and dedication to become a narcotics detective with the LAPD.

Throwing back the covers, she got out of bed and went to the bathroom to shower and change. It was the reading of the will today and the family lawyer was coming over. She wasn't looking forward to it, but he had been clear on the phone that they all needed to be there.

The pounding of the hot jets of water on her shoulders helped ease some of her tension but, after stepping out of the shower and drying herself off, the mirror told her that her face was still puffy from all the crying she had done the day before.

Hiding it as best she could under carefully applied make up, she got dressed. Not wanting to wear jeans for what was a formal occasion, she dressed in simple black pants with a short sleeved green blouse. Checking herself in the mirror a final time, she took a deep steadying breath and headed downstairs.

***

John Cassidy, the senior partner of the only law firm in town, was dressed formally in a dark suit and tie, and was seated behind the desk in the study while she, Jake and Carrie had taken chairs on the other side, facing him.

The atmosphere was relaxed, if somber, as they all knew what the will would contain. Kat didn't expect to receive anything, didn't want anything. In fact, she was quite happy with what she had. And, with Jamie missing, it was expected that the entire estate would pass to Jake. None of them saw this reading as anything other than a formality.

"How long is this going to take?" Carrie asked impatiently.

Kat had to bite her tongue. She'd only just met Jake's new wife, but she hadn't taken to her. She seemed hard, calculating even, and she hadn't shown any signs of grief at the loss of her in-laws. Surreptitiously glancing across at her now, Kat thought she looked excited, with not a trace of respect for the occasion on her features at all.

Mentally chiding herself for being so quick to judge, Kat pushed her thoughts aside. She knew nothing about her. There must be something about her to love or Jake would never have married her. It clearly just wasn't immediately obvious.

"If we're all ready, I'll get started," the lawyer said, ignoring Carrie's question.

The will was short and it didn't take long for him to read it through to the end. It was not at all what they had expected and when he had finished, there was complete silence in the room, a stunned silence from everyone. Carrie was the first to react.

"You've got to be shitting me!" she shouted. "They can't do that!"

"I assure you, madam, that the document is perfectly legal. I drew it up myself."

"Calm down, Carrie!" Jake hissed at her.

"Calm down? Calm the hell down? Didn't you hear what he just said?"

"He's right, Carrie, there's no need for that." Admittedly, the contents of the will had taken them all by surprise but she was totally overreacting.

Rather than leave everything to Jake, as they'd been expecting, all assets were to be held in a trust, managed by Kat. It was to remain that way until Jamie was found, alive or dead. At that time, it would either pass to them both, if she was found alive, or the entire estate would pass to Jake. Until that time, though, Kat was to look after everything, including the business, and keep it intact.

Turning to the lawyer, she smiled an apology for Carrie's outburst. "Thank you for coming. I'll see you out." Leaving the room and closing the door on the sound of Carrie and Jake arguing, she walked him through the house to the front door. "So, what happens now?"

"If you'd like to come to my office tomorrow, there are some documents I'll need you to sign." He slipped on his coat and opened the front door but didn't immediately leave. "I knew you and your sister as little girls. My daughter was in the same class as she was. You probably don't remember."

Kat shook her head. "No, I'm sorry. I don't."

"They met up again after you'd already left town and became good friends." He gave her a sad smile. "She knew that if anyone could find Jamie, you could. She was very proud of you."

The lump that formed in her throat made it impossible for her to speak and all she could do was watch as he left and got into his car, tears streaming down her face.

Nineteen

Two decades had passed since Kat had last seen him, but she knew that if she was going to do this, she was going to need his help. They'd been high school sweethearts, but she'd left town without even saying goodbye. She had no idea how he was going to react to seeing her now, and she was more nervous than she'd been about anything in years.

The local police station was an old, two-story building on the main road through the town. It looked just as it did when she'd been in high school, down to the 'E' in 'Police' being at an odd angle. She was just about to walk up the steps and through the front door when a voice stopped her in her tracks.

"So you're back, then?"

She turned around and there he was. Lounging against the side of his cruiser, hands in the pockets of his uniform pants.

God, she'd forgotten the effect he had on her; just looking at him again was making her stomach tie itself in knots and she wasn't entirely sure it was just because she was nervous. Time had been good to him and he obviously took care of himself. He could have passed for a man in his late twenties, not one approaching forty.

"Yes, it was the funeral today."

He nodded, the frown on his face softening. "Of course. I'm truly sorry for your loss. They were good folks."

"Thank you. Yes, they were." She waited, expecting him to say something, anything, about what had happened all those years ago, but he said nothing.

"So what are you doing here?" he asked casually, nodding towards the police station.

She was surprised. She wasn't sure what she'd expected, but it wasn't this, this casual conversation, as if they'd seen each other just last week. "I'm here about my niece, Jamie."

"Well, you'll probably want to speak to the chief about that. I think he's in his office. If you go in and speak to them at the desk, they'll point you in the right direction." He pushed himself off the cruiser and opened the door, preparing to get in. "It was good seeing you, Kat. Take care."

"Wait!" It came out as much more of a squeak than she'd intended.

He turned back towards her, waiting for her to speak. "It was you I came to see, Finn. I need your help." She took a deep breath. "You got time for a coffee?"

It felt as if he was looking directly into her soul as he looked at her with his chocolate brown eyes, clearly weighing up his answer. With a curt nod, he agreed. "There's a coffee shop across the street. I'll meet you there in fifteen minutes I've got a couple of jobs to do first." And without another word he got in the cruiser and drove off, leaving Kat standing there looking after him.

Glad that she had some time to pull herself together, she went in search of the coffee shop. She knew exactly where he meant, it had been a coffee shop when she'd lived here and Brecon Point was the kind of place that didn't change much.

Her reaction at seeing him had knocked her off balance. After all these years she had expected awkwardness, maybe some uncomfortable questions, but she hadn't expected the physical reaction she had felt.

She'd always regretted just leaving him without any kind of explanation but every time she'd been tempted to get in touch, she'd reminded herself that it was best for everyone involved if she didn't. Including him. She'd never meant to hurt him, but it would have hurt him far more if she'd stayed.

It felt strange walking down Main Street after all this time. Everything was familiar, and yet changed at the same time. The hairdresser was still where it had always been next to the grocery store, but the record shop where they'd all bought the latest music craze was gone, replaced with a garage workshop.

Finding the coffee shop exactly where it had always been, she went inside and took a booth at the back, ordering a coffee from the waitress who immediately appeared.

When he walked through the door exactly fifteen minutes later, she'd managed to re-group and was much more in control. She watched as he saw her, ordered a coffee at the counter then made his way over, sliding into the booth opposite her before speaking.

"So, you said you needed my help. What can I do for you?"

Kat searched his face for any sign that he was finding this as awkward as she, was but there was nothing. It was completely expressionless. He could have been sitting across the table from anybody. Well, that suited her; she was here for his help, not a trip down memory lane.

"Yes, I did." She had intended to apologize, to try and explain, but it appeared there was no need. "I've got to find Jamie, one way or another, and I need your help to do it."

The waitress picked that moment to come over with his coffee, cutting off his reply, and she was surprised at the stab of jealousy she felt when he winked at her as he said, "Thanks."

"Friend of yours?" she asked after she'd left, before she could stop the sarcastic remark slipping off her tongue.

He raised his eyebrows, looking amused. "You do know that the entire police department has been looking for her since she disappeared, don't you? We haven't given up."

"I know, and I'm truly grateful for all the efforts that have been put in. It's just that it's become a bit more imperative that we find out once and for all what happened to her." She went on to explain about the will. "So, you see why I need to find her."

"I'm still confused. What do you think you can do that we haven't?"

She sighed and, wrapping her hands around her cup, decided to just be honest. "I don't know, I really don't. But I do know I have to try. I was a lousy sister, and I've been a lousy aunt. I owe them this."

"Okay. I get that." He nodded "But I still don't know where I fit in."

"You have the contacts. I've been gone for twenty years and I don't know people around here anymore. And you were here when she disappeared, and afterwards. You'll be able to give me a lot more than I'll get just looking at the paperwork, presuming the chief will even let me see it."

He was quiet for a long time, just sipping his coffee, before he finally looked up and met her eyes. "Okay, I'll help. But just to be clear, I'm not doing this for you. I'm doing it because it's the right thing to do and I've always thought there was something odd about the way she vanished." He drained his cup. "I'll go and clear it with the chief. I've been pushing to look at the case again so, I'm sure he'll agree if only to shut me up. I'll meet you back here tomorrow morning at 9 a.m. sharp.

Don't be late." And without another word, he stood up and left, without looking back.

She spent what was left of the afternoon at the lawyer's office signing all the papers, effectively giving her control of the business and the family assets with immediate effect. She hadn't anticipated this when she'd come back, and the responsibility weighed heavily on her as she got in her car to drive home.

It was dusk when she finally turned the rental car onto the drive leading up to the house. It still felt strange, despite having been back a couple of days now, driving up to the house again. She been born here, had grown up here with her sister, and this was the last place that she'd ever seen her parents. And would now be the last place she'd ever seen her sister.

After she'd left, her sister had told her that her parents had completely cut her out of their will so, when they'd died, the house and the business had passed to her, though the running of it was left to her husband. Kat had had no issue with that. This house, this town, held only bad memories for her and she'd wanted no part of it.

As a trustee of the estate now though, she had a legal responsibility to look after it and the business until Jamie was found. *The sooner you find her, the sooner you can pack up and get out of here,* she thought to herself as she pulled her car to a stop outside the front door.

Letting herself in, she could hear Jake and Carrie arguing in the living room through the closed door. Since she'd arrived, that's all they'd done. *They certainly didn't seem to like each other very much for a couple that were only recently married,* she thought to herself.

Not sure she was feeling up to getting caught in the middle of an argument, she debated going straight upstairs to her room and leaving them to it, but she couldn't. She had a feeling that Jake could probably use her support. As she went to open the living room door, it was flung open and Carrie stormed out, nearly knocking her over.

Concerned, Kat poked her head around the door. "Everything okay?" Jake stood by the fire with his hands in his pockets, looking thoroughly miserable.

"Yeah. She's just a bit highly-strung." He shrugged and looked at her apologetically.

That's not quite how I would describe her, she thought, but kept it to herself, instead saying, "How are you coping?"

He sighed. "I'm okay, I guess. What hurts the most is that we didn't find Jamie before they died." He looked over at her, and Kat could see he was tormented. "You know that Dad and I never really got along, but even so I wouldn't have wished this on anyone."

Going to him, she placed her hand on his arm. "I know that. And I'm so sorry I didn't come sooner. I should have. I'll never forgive myself for that." She felt tears fill her eyes and then spill down her cheeks.

Jake took a step towards her and pulled her to him in a bear hug and she allowed herself to cry. "You're here now, that's all that matters."

Reluctantly pulling away, she wiped her eyes. She reminded herself that she had a job to do. "Well, we can't give up. We can still bring her home." Turning, she walked to the couch and sat down, indicating that he should do the same. "I spoke to a friend of mine in town today, and he's going to help me look." She saw the doubtful expression on his face, but before he could say anything she held up her hand. "I know, I know, the police have already looked. But they might have missed something."

He still didn't look convinced. "Aunt Kat, they spent months looking for her, I doubt you'll be able to find her, much as I'd like to think you could."

Kat refused to consider failure as an option, so she wasn't about to let Jake see that she had exactly the same doubts. Smiling brightly, she told him, "The difference between us and the police is that we're much more motivated." Reaching for a glass decanter and matching glasses that sat on the coffee table, she poured them both a drink. "So, tell me everything you can remember about that day, however unimportant you think it is."

He hated lying to Kat, but he couldn't tell her everything. The police had never found out about

Jamie's visit to Carrie and that they'd had a fight and she'd left there very upset. They'd decided there was no need to tell them, it wasn't relevant to her disappearance. He'd wanted to initially, but Carrie had convinced him that opening that particular door would have led to increased scrutiny and he couldn't risk them finding out about Ted. It was yet another thing that just the two of them were aware of, and it had to stay that way.

Recounting the events of the day now, though, brought it all back. When Jamie had first vanished, he'd thought that she'd simply run off for a few days, upset by what she'd found out. But when she'd failed to return, he hadn't known what to think.

As the days turned to weeks, and then months, and he saw what it was doing to his parents, he was ashamed. Ashamed of how badly he'd treated them. Watching their pain, and feeling his own, they'd developed a new closeness, one that had never been there before.

Rather than fade with time, what he had done to Ted increasingly preyed on his mind and the knowledge that it was all due to his greed made him sick.

Twenty

Slamming the bedroom door behind her after storming out of the living room and going upstairs, Carrie threw herself on their bed. She was furious. She had worked so damned hard to get here and now it could all be snatched away from her! And Jake couldn't understand what she was so upset about. He didn't seem remotely bothered that he couldn't claim his inheritance until his damned sister showed up. She tried to make herself breathe slowly while she stared at the ceiling, hoping it would help her calm down.

His parents had taken a lot of convincing when he'd told them that they wanted to get married. They didn't like her, but it was the fact that they wanted to go ahead even though Jamie was missing that they'd seemed to find so offensive.

She'd wanted to get that ring on her finger as soon as she could, though, so she'd pushed Jake continuously, until he'd agreed that they would go ahead with or without his parents' permission. What choice did he have? He knew that she could, and would, have told the police about his involvement in Ted's death if he didn't. Luckily, the mere threat that they would go ahead anyway had been enough to get them to agree. So, six months after Jamie's disappearance, they'd finally tied the knot.

She had to admit, she'd expected to be in for a much longer wait before she saw the benefit of marrying him but his parents getting killed like that had been a stroke of luck. Jake was devastated, of course, and she was playing the part of the bereaved daughter-in-law, but secretly she was elated. At last, she was lady of the manor. People would have to look up to her now, show her the proper respect.

But now everything was spoiled. It could be years before she got her hands on any money.

They'd just had another argument about it. He'd changed since Jamie had gone. She'd thought he had more backbone, wanted the same things she did, but he was soft, kept whining about how much he missed his sister. It was all she could do to stop herself blurting out the truth, that his precious sister was gone for good. But she knew that even Jake wouldn't let that slide, even though he'd end up in prison himself for what he had done to Ted.

She'd known what she needed to do as soon as the will had been read. Jamie needed to be found. D*ead* or alive.

Twenty-One

Letting himself into his house on the outskirts of town, he slammed the front door harder than he should have, making a picture fall off the wall and smash on the floor. Cursing, he picked it up and carried it to the kitchen, dumping it in the kitchen sink. He was angry at himself. And her. How dare she just waltz back into town and then act as if nothing had happened? And more to the point, how the hell had he just let her?

He'd known it was her standing outside the station the moment he'd spotted her. He hadn't known whether she would come back for her sister's funeral as she'd missed her own parents, but it had always been a possibility.

She was still stunning, even after all these years. She'd always been slim and he could see that she'd kept her figure and she still kept her gorgeous, dark hair long, hanging half way down her back.

The anger he still felt towards her had surprised him. It had been years since she'd so unceremoniously walked out of his life and he'd thought that he'd forgiven her, if not forgotten. It had taken a bit of time, but he'd moved on and met someone else. They were long divorced now but he'd believed that that episode of his life had been firmly left in the past.

Sitting across from her in the coffee shop, he'd wanted to demand answers, but he had his pride so he'd kept quiet. Being close to her again was going to be hard but he'd committed to helping her now and he would be true to his word. Besides, what he'd told her had been true. He had always thought there was something odd about Jamie's disappearance, coming so soon as it did after the murder of her fiancé.

The whole department had been involved in the search, but no trace of her had ever been found. Her abandoned car had been forensically examined, but it had revealed nothing.

Deciding that he needed to work off some of this frustration, he went upstairs and changed into a pair of dark blue overalls before heading out to the garage. As always, he got a thrill when he switched on the bright overhead lights that revealed his pride and joy: a sea green, 1967 Pontiac GTO.

He'd discovered it abandoned in a barn during a case a few years before. When he'd contacted the owner of the barn, he'd been happy to sell it to him for a few hundred dollars. When he'd bought it, it had been hardly more than a shell, but over the past few years he had been painstakingly restoring it to its former glory. He'd found that when he was working on it he was able to focus entirely and put all other thoughts from his mind. He needed that oblivion now so, after switching the radio on to the local country and western channel, he closed the door and got to work.

Twenty-Two

She'd pretended to be asleep that morning when Jake left, not at all in the mood to deal with him. Once she was sure he was gone, she'd jumped out of bed wanting to get an early start. She needed to dress appropriately for what she had planned so she threw on an old pair of blue jeans, a plain navy blue t-shirt, and some hiking boots.

Avoiding Kat, she headed downstairs and straight out the front door without even stopping for breakfast. There was a gas station on the way out of town, she would stop there and grab a coffee. Apart from anything else, the task ahead was likely to be quite gruesome and she thought it would probably be best tackled on an empty stomach.

She'd left her deep in the woods, in the middle of nowhere, so no one was likely to just stumble upon her bones. Even she wasn't sure if she'd be able to remember exactly where. She'd better remember though, and quick; she had no intention of waiting any longer than she had to for what was rightfully hers.

After grabbing a coffee, it took her nearly an hour of driving around until she spotted a familiar dirt track. She followed it as far as she could in her car and then stopped when she could go no further.

Getting out, she went to the trunk and removed the roll of industrial garbage bags and thick gardening gloves she had gathered the night before and slammed the trunk shut. With a quick look around to make sure she was alone, she followed the track further into the forest.

She remembered that night as if it were yesterday. After finding Jamie by the side of the road near her broken down car, she'd offered her a lift. Despite the argument they'd just had, Jamie had known that if she didn't accept she could have been stuck there for hours so, reluctantly, she'd gotten in.

She hadn't been expecting Carrie to strike her with a blow to the head with the tire iron she kept under the driver's seat. She'd still been conscious, so she'd hit her again and she'd gone still. It hadn't been planned, so she'd had to drive for miles until she'd found the dirt track which had led to these woods.

Jamie had started to come around as she'd dragged her out of the car, so she'd had to hit her a few more times to make sure she wouldn't wake up again, ever. It had been incredibly hard, backbreaking work dragging her through the forest by her arms until she'd found a spot where she'd been happy that no one would ever find her.

She'd never expected to have to come back here, but now she had no choice. If she wanted to get her hands on the money, Jamie's body needed to be found and it wouldn't be found out here. That's what the bags were for. She planned on gathering up her bones and then moving them to somewhere where they would quickly be stumbled upon.

It took a while, but eventually she started getting her bearings and recognizing landmarks: the big stone shaped like a saucer, and the tree that looked like a fork. It had been dark when she'd left her here and she'd made a note of these things so she'd be able to make her way back to the car.

Finally she came to the place where she'd left her. She didn't feel squeamish at all. After all this time, the only thing left would be bones. She was sure of that.

She'd been searching for a quarter of an hour before she started panicking. *Where the hell was she?* She should have found her by now. Even allowing for the passage of time and interference by wild animals, she should have found some remains.

Eyes glued to the ground, she kicked long-fallen leaves aside with her boots, stopping occasionally to get a closer look at something that looked promising, but turned out to be nothing. Expanding her search in ever widening circles, her actions became increasingly frantic when she still found no trace of Jamie. She didn't stop until the sweat on her skin started to cool and she looked up through the tree canopy, and realizing that the sun was going down. Not wanting to get lost out here at night, she reluctantly headed back to her car.

***

Carrie's mind was racing as she sat, catching her breath, trying not to let the panic overwhelm her. Jamie had been dead when she left her there, she was sure of it. And besides, if she'd still been alive she would have made her way home, and her ass would be in jail right now not here searching the woods. So, that left two explanations. One, she'd not been dead and had managed to somehow move away from where she'd left her and died somewhere else, or the animals had scattered her bones so thoroughly that none remained. Neither scenario was good news for her. How the hell was she going to get her hands on the money now?

Twenty-Three

Not again. Belle's heart sank as she rounded the corner and saw the blue and red flashing lights. There were so many and they reflected in the puddles of water on the streets left after the earlier rain shower, making it appear that the whole street was awash with them. As she drew closer, she could see the yellow police tape cordoning off an alley between two buildings and the press clamouring as they tried to get closer, angry at being held back.

Seeing a small group of the regular girls standing to one side, she pulled her coat tight around her and hurried over.

"Another one?" She knew the answer before anyone spoke and her fears were confirmed.

"Jasmine." It was Sue who spoke, one of the older ladies who had been working the streets for as long as anyone could remember.

"Oh, God, no! She was just a kid!" Belle had met her a couple of times. She couldn't have been more than about seventeen. "Do they think it's him again?"

"They haven't said, but I found her, I saw what he did. It's the same guy."

The rest of the group murmured their agreement. Belle didn't ask what he'd done; she didn't need to. This was the eighth working girl to be murdered in the last four months, and always the same way. They were sexually assaulted, their throats slit, and then they were propped up, naked, against a wall. Just thinking about it now made her pull her coat tighter around her. They were all living in fear that they might be next.

A blinding, bright light suddenly hit her face and she had to hold up her arm to shield her eyes to see. It was one of the cameramen from the press, standing next to one of the female anchors from the local news station.

"Ladies, did you know the victim?" She didn't bother waiting for an answer. "Do you feel safe being out here at night?" She shoved her microphone towards them, waiting for an answer.

Ignoring it, Belle turned and walked away quickly. Blade had spent so long drumming it into her that she must avoid her picture being taken that now it was second nature. The last thing she wanted was for anyone to see her and to be arrested for murder. She'd seen enough; she was done for tonight and if Blade didn't like it, well, it was just tough. Business would be quiet now anyway, most of the customers scared off by the police presence. She might as well make the most of it and get an early night.

Twenty-Four

Kat hadn't slept very well, tossing and turning most of the night. She'd had vivid dreams in which Finn had featured quite heavily and not always fully clothed. She felt the heat fill her cheeks again as she remembered them.

Your sister is dead and your niece is missing and you're having sexy dreams? She was chiding herself as his shadow fell across the table. Feeling as if she'd been caught doing something she shouldn't, she felt her cheeks get even brighter as she looked up and found Finn standing there. The smirk he gave her told her that he had noticed her discomfort and seemed to find it amusing.

"We meet again," he drawled at her as he took a seat.

"Hardly surprising, since we agreed we'd meet here," she snapped, cross with herself for letting him get to her.

"Yes, but you're hardly known for doing what you agree to, are you?" he responded, reminding her again of their shared past.

Taking a deep breath, she ignored the comment and pulled a notebook and pencil out of her purse. "Okay, I was thinking last night that the best thing to do would probably be to go over things from the beginning. I wasn't here so I don't know what steps the locals took. That way, we can see if they missed anything or if there's anything worth going over again."

"Hold your horses. I haven't had any breakfast yet and, if we're going to do this, I'm not doing it on an empty stomach or in a public place." He signaled to the waitress. "We'll have something to eat and then I'll take you over to the impound yard. We still have the car over there and I thought you might want to take a look."

He was right, of course. There was no point going off half-cocked. It was probably best to get a picture of the crime scene in her mind before going into too much detail. "Okay, that makes sense." Though for some reason, it pained her to admit he was right. "I'll have what you're having."

She put the pad back in her purse and sat back, looking at him as he ordered. He hadn't changed much. His face was still ruggedly handsome with the strong, square jaw that she remembered. There were a few more lines on his face than there had been then, but the same could be said of her. He was keeping his hair shorter, too, though it was still dark and thick.

"So what happened to college? I thought you were going to become a lawyer and lock up all the bad guys?" That had been part of the reason she had left, so that she didn't destroy his dream. She'd been surprised when her sister had told her that he'd never left town.

"Things don't always turn out the way you expect them to, do they?" He seemed to realize he spoken harshly and immediately apologized. "Look, I'm sorry, but you asked for my help and you've got it, but I'm not here to reminisce, okay?"

Hurt, Kat just nodded and concentrated on eating her food. He was right; she had no right to expect that they could be friends.

They finished their breakfast in silence before heading over to the impound lot. It was really not much more than a fenced in yard around the back of the police station and her niece's car was the only occupant. She was surprised to see that it wasn't being kept under cover and had been left out in the elements. "Why hasn't it been preserved as a crime scene?"

"CSI went over every inch of it. There was nothing more they could do."

She wasn't at all happy with that. If they had missed anything, it was likely lost now. "We wouldn't have done that in L.A.. It would have been kept preserved as evidence until the case was solved."

"You're not in L.A., though, are you? You're in Hicksville," he snapped as he turned and walked out of the lot.

Walking fast to catch up with him, she grabbed his arm and pulled him to a stop. "I'm sorry. I didn't mean that to come out the way it did." She took a deep breath. "I just need to find her. She and Jake are the only family I've got left."

He nodded. "Come on, then. I'll take you to where we found the car."

She resolved to actually think about what she was saying before opening her mouth in the future and followed him to his car.

***

The location had been disappointing. It was in the middle of nowhere and there was absolutely nothing to see. It didn't help that Finn had hardly said two words to her since they had left the diner. She was feeling quite down as they drove back towards town and she rested her head against the glass of the passenger window, watching the fields as they sped past. She had been sitting like that for a few miles and had given up on the idea of conversation when he did actually speak.

"My dad lost his job."

She looked at him quizzically, confused by what he had said.

"You asked why I didn't go to college. Well, Dad lost his job and we couldn't afford the tuition and there was no chance of me getting a scholarship." He kept his eyes on the road as he said this, not giving anything away.

"I'm so sorry. I know how much it meant to you."

"You'd be surprised how little anything meant to me after you left," he said, the bitterness plain in his voice.

She didn't know how to respond. Part of her heart was flying to hear that he'd cared so much, but a bigger part was breaking to know that she'd done that to him.

"Finn…"

He didn't let her finish. "Don't. It's in the past. I moved on, met someone else. It's all history now."

They didn't speak again until he dropped her back at her car. "I think we've done enough for today. I've got some errands to run this afternoon so I'll pick up the case files from the station and we can get together again tomorrow to go through them."

"Shall we meet at the coffee shop again?"

"No, the files are confidential. We can't go over them in public. Come to my place just after lunch." He wrote his address down on a piece of paper and handed it to her through the window.

"Ok, see you then."

***

With the rest of the afternoon free, Kat decided it was probably about time she visited the office. The business had been in their family for generations and she used to go to there sometimes with her mother when they were small to visit her father.

It was hard to think of her parents. When she'd left, the only way she'd been able to cope was to not think about them. If she did, her grief overwhelmed her. Because that's what it had felt like, grief. They'd still been alive, but they'd made it clear that she was no longer their daughter. She had kept in touch with her sister without their knowledge and she knew that her mother had asked about her, but her father never spoke her name again.

The plant was about ten miles out of town and spread over several acres in several distinct buildings. The business used to exclusively supply parts for the automotive industry but with that industry's general decline, it had expanded and now had several arms. Not only did they still supply car manufacturers, but now they supplied parts to the maritime industry and carried out defense contract work, some of it highly classified. It was the single biggest local employer, with most of the population of Brecon point either working there or having a family member who did.

Jake had been in charge since his father was killed and she had no intention of interfering with that. She'd have no idea where to start anyway, but she did need to familiarize herself with the day-to-day running if she was to take her new responsibilities seriously.

She spent the rest of the afternoon sifting through mountains of paperwork in the office space Jake had made available for her, close to his. She was pleased that he did not seem resentful at all of her presence; it could so easily have been a difficult situation.

By the time the sun went down, she was exhausted and her eyeballs hurt from too much reading. *No arguments tonight!* She was just too tired to get caught in the middle of another row between Jake and Carrie and resolved to go straight home, take a long hot bath, read a book and get an early night.

Twenty-Five

The morning was spent catching up on phone calls and paperwork. Her first call had been to her captain back in L.A., asking for a bit more time off. She'd worked incredibly hard to regain his trust after disappearing to London and hadn't taken a day off until it had been forced on her. This meant that she had a lot of holiday time owed to her and he was happy for her to take as long as she needed, which was a relief. She didn't want to have to be worrying about whether she had a job to go back to, as well as everything else.

The next call had been to Kyle and Tara. Kyle was her old partner, and it was for him that she'd dropped everything and jetted off to London two years ago. He'd gone to rescue Tara from the clutches of her boss, who'd used her as a prize in his underground poker games. She'd refused to let him go alone and they'd managed to track her down and bring her and her long-lost daughter home.

She'd promised them that she'd keep them up to date with what was happening, so she'd filled them in on the contents of the will. She hadn't told them that she was planning on looking for Jamie herself as she knew full well that they'd be on the first plane down here to help and she didn't want to drag them away from L.A.

Besides, their P.I. company had taken off and they were far too busy to take the time away. They'd come anyway, she knew that, but she wasn't prepared to put them in that position. They had a spare key to her place and they'd promised to go in periodically, just to check everything was all right.

Getting up from the kitchen table, Kat went to the counter to make herself another cup of coffee. It really was a sad reflection on her life that she could drop everything and walk away so easily. There was no one who needed her, who would even miss her. Not even a cat. The thought did nothing for her mood, which was low that morning anyway.

For years she'd held the fact that she'd done the right thing all those years ago close to her heart. It had helped her get past the nights when she'd cried herself to sleep, when the ache within her had almost been too much to bear. Since she'd been back, though, she'd started to see things through different eyes. Would it have been so awful if she'd stayed? Seeing that Finn was happy despite not pursuing his dream threw a shadow of doubt over her that hadn't been there before, and she didn't like it.

Realizing that she'd been staring into her coffee until it had gone cold, she checked the clock on the wall. Past one. Feeling selfish for wallowing in thoughts of herself, she pushed them aside and brought her attention back to what she had to do today.

She was hoping that going through the files might throw up something, anything, that may give them a clue. She'd seen it happen many times; a case gone completely cold until looked at with a pair of fresh eyes. Something looked at so many times that it didn't stand out and got missed.

Jake and Carrie were both out, so she locked the door behind her as she left and climbed into her car. She had to go through town to get to the address Finn had given her so she stopped at the coffee shop and got them both a coffee on the way.

She could see as soon as she pulled up outside the address Finn had given her that the house was well cared for. It wasn't large, a typical two bed, two bath with a small yard out front and larger yard out back. The grass was neatly mowed and it looked as if the house had not long ago had a new coat of paint.

It occurred to her as she walked up the path to the front door that she hadn't asked if he lived here alone. Suddenly feeling awkward, she knocked on the door. There was nothing but silence from the other side, so she knocked again. Still nothing. *He wouldn't have forgotten would he?*

Walking back down the path she noticed the garage at the side of the house and walked towards it. As she drew closer, she could hear the unmistakable sound of country and western coming from behind the garage door.

Knocking on it loudly so she could be heard above the music, she heard it stop before the garage door was pushed open. Finn stood there, covered in oil with a wrench in his hand. Behind him was one of the most beautiful cars she'd ever seen.

"Is that what I think it is?" she asked, walking towards the car. "A 1967 Pontiac GTO?" She walked around it admiringly. "Didn't you have a poster of one of these on your bedroom wall in high school?" She remembered it; it had had the prized place above his bed.

"You remember that?" he asked, wiping his oily hands on a rag before taking the coffee she was holding out to him. "Thanks."

She just nodded, not trusting herself to speak. There were many things she remembered about his bedroom back then.

"Come on in the house." He closed the garage door and led her through a side door into the kitchen. "I'll go wash up. Make yourself at home. The living room is through there." He pointed to a door just down the hall before disappearing upstairs and leaving her alone.

The house was nicely decorated in neutral colors, but it still managed to feel warm and welcoming, partly due to the clever use of accent colors but also because of the many pictures adorning the walls. They were all along the walls in the hall, and when she went into the living room, she saw that they were on the walls there, too. Taking a closer look she could see that they were pictures of family and friends in various settings. On vacation, rock climbing, by the beach, even one of Finn sitting astride a surf board, smiling for the camera.

She couldn't help but wonder who had taken that picture. A girlfriend? There were no obvious signs that anyone else lived in the house though. Kat wasn't entirely sure why, but that made her feel better.

She didn't have long to dwell on the question as she heard Finn coming down the stairs, and a moment later he appeared in the doorway. Gone were the overalls, replaced by jeans and a clean t-shirt and his hair was still damp from the shower.

"Right. I'm all yours." He smiled. "I've put all the files in the dining room so we can use the table to spread out."

Following him, she saw a single cardboard box on the dining room table. She was pleased to see that it was full, telling her that a lot of work had been put into the case. Taking seats on opposite sides of the table, they split the contents of the box between them and got to work.

***

Over the next few hours, they pored over every single piece of paper that the investigation had generated so far. They painstakingly went over all the statements that had been taken, all the forensic reports and all the interview transcripts from people they'd questioned about her disappearance and found nothing.

"Someone must have seen something!" Kat cried, throwing the document she was reading down on the table.

Looking up from his own reading, Finn could see that the frustration was getting to her. "Look, why don't we take a break?" he stood up from the table. "We've been at this for hours, we've earned it. There's a deck out back, I'll grab us a beer."

He'd pretty much expected that they wouldn't find anything in the files. He'd gone through them enough times himself, and though he was no high and mighty L.A. detective, he was a good cop and he was sure he would have spotted anything they'd missed. She needed to see that for herself, though, and he understood that. She'd never be able to move on until she'd done everything she could.

Taking two cold beers from the fridge, he carried them out to the deck where Kat was already sitting. It was just after five, and though the sun was going down, it was still warm in the late afternoon sun. Handing her one of the beers, he lowered himself into the unoccupied deck chair. Neither of them spoke for a few minutes, sitting in companionable silence, sipping their beers.

"What do you think happened to her?"

He looked over at her but she wasn't looking at him; she was looking into the distance. "I don't know, I really don't."

"You must have some ideas, though? What does your gut tell you?" She turned and looked at him now and he could see the need for answers in her eyes.

He wasn't sure she wanted to hear the answer to that question, but he needed to be honest. "I think she walked away."

"What?" She turned to face him, her voice betraying her anger. "You really believe that? So what's all this, then? Going through the files, showing me the car. Humoring me?"

"Kat, calm down and hear me out, will you?" He'd known his opinion wouldn't be popular. "Look, everything points to it. Her fiancé had not long before been murdered, there was absolutely no sign of a struggle and according to just about everyone we spoke to, she didn't have any enemies."

Kat was shaking her head. "No. No way. She wasn't that kind of girl. She would never have just walked away from her life and not let her folks know she was okay, never."

"You did." He regretted it the moment the words left his lips and he saw the flash of anger in her eyes.

"What? How dare you?" She was breathing hard now. "I walked away, yes, for a damned good reason. And my family knew exactly where I was. It's not the same thing at all." She stood up. "This hasn't been about helping me find Jamie at all has it? It's been about you getting your kicks because your macho pride is still hurt because I walked out on you."

"Don't be ridiculous. If you'd just calm down, you'd see what I'm saying makes sense."

"I'll see myself out." She turned and went back into the house.

He watched as she went, slamming the porch door behind her, and debated whether to follow. Deciding it was best just to let her calm down, he remained on the deck long after he'd heard her car start up and pull away, the squeal of her tires telling him it might be a while before she did.

She had been wrong, though. That wasn't why he thought the way he did. There simply wasn't any evidence pointing to foul play. He truly did want to help her, but she needed to accept that she may not like what they discovered. If they discovered anything at all.

I should have just said no, he thought to himself. It would have been much easier if he'd just told her to deal with the chief directly. He was glad he had company coming over tonight. He really didn't want to spend time analyzing his reasons for saying yes again. He wasn't sure he'd like the result.

Twenty-Six

She was still pissed, but the fire had gone from her anger. She'd spent the evening slamming her way around the house and even Carrie had had the good sense to avoid her. In the mood she was in, she would have gone for the jugular.

She had no idea why she'd reacted as strongly as she had but, if she was honest with herself, she figured it probably had something to do with the guilt she felt. Being in this place again was too much. This was exactly why she'd never come back. She needed to get out of here as soon as she could and get back to her own life. It may not be a particularly full one, but at least she wasn't on an emotional roller coaster all the time.

The house was quiet now as she padded back upstairs with a glass of hot milk. She'd had it as a child when she couldn't sleep and thought she'd give it a try. It was nearly 3 a.m. and she hadn't slept a wink, even though she was so tired her bones ached.

Propping herself up in bed, she settled back to watch the news. They were showing a special report about a suspected serial killer in the next state. The hot milk nearly scalded her as she spilled it down herself, leaping out of bed. *It was her!* It had only been a few seconds, but there was no doubt in her mind. *Jamie had been in that broadcast!*

For a moment, she didn't know what to do, shocked by what she had just seen. She wanted to run and wake up Jake and tell him that his sister was alive, but what if she was wrong? No, she couldn't raise his hopes like that.

Immediately, she thought of Finn. She had to speak to Finn. *Shit!* She'd never gotten his cellphone number. She very briefly considered waiting until morning, but that thought was quickly pushed aside. This couldn't wait until then; she had to see him now.

Throwing on a pair of jeans and a sweater, she ran down the stairs as quietly as she could. If she woke Jake and Carrie up, they'd want to know where she was going in the middle of the night and she couldn't tell them, not yet.

The roads were deserted as she drove way over the speed limit in her hurry to get there, replaying what she'd seen in her mind. She was absolutely sure it was her. She looked different, and she'd been dressed like a hooker, but it was her. She was sure of it.

Pulling her car to a stop outside Finn's house, all thoughts of what had happened earlier long gone, she banged on his door. She'd been banging for what felt like ages before a light went on upstairs. She heard someone on the other side of the door and saw a shadow fall across the peephole. The door opened and Finn stood there in his shorts, his hair rumpled from where he'd been sleeping.

"Kat? It's the middle of the night! What's wrong?" He rubbed his eyes.

Trying to keep her eyes averted from his naked chest, the words tumbled out of her mouth. "She's alive! Jamie! She's alive!" She walked past him into the house. "I saw her on TV. I know it was her!"

"Whoa, slow down!" He took hold of her arms to get her to stand still "What on earth are you talking about?"

"I was watching TV just now and I saw her!"

"Is everything okay?" Kat spun round at the sound of a female voice. About halfway up the stairs stood a woman, wearing nothing but a man's shirt. She was quite beautiful, with long red, curly hair and a great pair of legs, from what she could see.

Suddenly, she felt incredibly foolish. What had she been thinking, coming over here in the middle of the night? It had never occurred to her that he wouldn't be alone, though she didn't know why.

"Shit. I'm sorry, I don't know what I was thinking." She couldn't look at Finn. "Look, I'll come back in the morning. I'm so sorry." She had her hand on the door handle when Finn stopped her.

"Kat, its fine. Isn't it, babe?" He addressed the woman on the stairs. "You don't mind, do you? It's work."

"Of course I don't. I'll go back to bed. Nice to meet you." She offered to Kat before turning and going back up the stairs.

Finn led her into the living room before closing the door gently and turning to her. "Now, what's this all about?"

Taking a deep breath and trying to explain properly this time, Kat told him what she'd seen on the news a short time ago.

"Are you sure? It's the middle of the night. You're tired and, understandably, a bit emotional at the moment."

She could hear the doubt in his voice and it irritated her. "Don't patronize me. I may be tired and emotional, but I'm still a highly trained detective. My brain hasn't turned to mush. I know what I saw and it was her."

He looked her in the eye and she met his gaze unwaveringly. For a few moments they remained like that, eyes locked, before he spoke again. "Okay. I believe you. Well, there's nothing we can do tonight so we should both try and get some sleep. We can look into it first thing in the morning."

Like she was going to get any sleep now! She should have just waited until it was light before charging round here, but she'd been so shocked that she'd just needed to tell him right away. "Yes. Of course, you're right. Please apologize to your friend for me."

"There's nothing to apologize for. This is wonderful news. Don't worry, okay?" He took hold of her upper arms, looking into her eyes "we'll find her."

***

She watched as the lights downstairs went off before she started her engine. Seeing that woman on the stairs had come as a shock, though she had no idea why. *Did she honestly think that he'd spent the last twenty years pining for her?* She had no claim on him, but her own feelings were betraying her.

She'd needed his help but she could take it from here. She needed to distance herself from him. Being this close wasn't healthy. She'd thought she'd be able to handle it, but she was wrong.

The news broadcast had been filmed in Parkway. If she left now, she could be there by breakfast time. She just needed to swing by the house, pack a few things and leave a note for Jake. She would just tell him that she was following up on a lead, where she was headed and that she would be in touch as soon as she had any news.

With one last look at the house, she put the car in drive and drove off.

Twenty-Seven

Apart from a couple of coffee and bathroom stops, she'd driven through the night and had arrived at Parkway's local TV station at just after 8 a.m.

She knew she was right, but what Finn had said last night had been nagging at her constantly on the drive. What if she was wrong and it was wishful thinking? She needed to be sure before she went off on a wild goose chase, and the only way to do that was going to the source.

Leaving her car in the parking lot out front, she went inside. The TV station was one of the smaller local stations and was situated in an older building away from the center of town where the other, bigger, stations were based. A bored security guard manned the reception desk, and when she asked to see someone about the broadcast he lazily waved his hand towards an elevator to his left and told her to go to the third floor.

Stepping out, she looked around, unsure who to speak to. The whole floor was open with cubicles dotted around, many already occupied even at this early hour. No one paid her any attention as she spotted an enclosed office in the far corner and made her way over to it.

A harassed-looking man waved her in impatiently when she knocked, barely glancing in her direction.

"Hi. I wonder if you can help me."

"Who are you?" He looked at her, a puzzled expression on his face. "Do you work here?"

"No, I've come about a news broadcast you showed last night." She held out her hand. "My name is Kat Mckay."

He took her outstretched hand. "I'm sorry. Everyone is supposed to be met in reception. I'll have to speak to Gus about that he shouldn't have just sent you up. I'm John Flint. I'm in charge around here. How can I help you?"

Kat explained what she'd come for.

"And you think your missing niece was captured on the broadcast? Okay, well there's one way to find out for sure." He stood up. "Follow me and I'll take you down to the production office. They'll be able to show you a tape of the show and you can find out either way."

After explaining what she needed and wishing her luck, John left her in the production office. It took a few minutes for them to bring up the broadcast and her stomach was in knots by the time they indicated that it was ready.

Taking a seat in front of one of the many screens in the room, she held her breath as the technician pressed play. "Stop it there!" she said when they were a couple of minutes into the tape. Frozen on the screen was her niece. There was absolutely no doubt about it.

"Can I get a copy of the tape?"

"Yep, sure," the technician replied, and quickly made her a copy before handing her a disc.

Thanking him, she quickly made her way back out of the building to her car. Though she was exhausted from being up most of the night, she didn't have time to rest. She needed to get this tape to the police as soon as possible.

***

She'd felt excited and hopeful on the way over to the Parkway P.D. building, in downtown Parkway. Those feelings had quickly dissipated, though, and now she was growing increasingly frustrated with the detective that had taken her into a side room to listen to her story. One thing was for sure, she was getting a better understanding of the victims of crime she dealt with must feel. Usually she was on the other side of the table, the one asking the questions. Now, though, she was at the mercy of the great lump of a man sitting opposite her who didn't seem in any hurry to get anything done to find Jamie.

"Okay, just so I understand, do you mind if we run through it one more time from the top?" he asked, speaking to her as if she were some kind of half wit.

"Yes, I do mind!" She had tried to stay calm, repeating it twice already, but now she was losing her cool. "I've told you everything I know. All you have to do is get in touch with Brecon Point police and they will fill you in on all the details I haven't covered. Now, can we please get out there and start looking for my niece?"

"It's not that simple, I'm afraid." He even seemed to speak in slow motion. Looking at his wide girth, she suspected he did everything in slow motion. "We have to do everything through the proper channels." He picked up his pad where he had been scribbling notes as she filled him in on the case. "Leave it with me and I'll be in touch as soon as I can. Is there a number I can get you on?"

Not trusting herself to speak, Kat scribbled her cell number down on the bottom of the pad he was holding out to her and, without another word, turned and walked out. *What a waste of time that was!* She was fuming. If he thought she had come all this way just to sit around and wait until they decided to do something, they were wrong.

There wasn't much more she could do for now, and the overnight drive was taking its toll. She could barely keep her eyes open. She'd spotted a hotel not far from the police station on her way into town, so she headed there now. After checking in, she took the elevator to her room and let herself in.

Knowing that it was unlikely that combing the streets at this time of the morning would do any good, she decided to get some sleep and start looking once it got dark. She would spend every night walking every street in town if he had to. Holding on to that thought, she just about managed to get herself undressed and climb under the cool, crisp covers of the bed before falling into a deep and blissfully dreamless sleep.

Twenty-Eight

He was pissed. *Damn that stubborn woman!* When he hadn't heard from her by midday, he'd driven up to the house to find her. It had been Carrie who'd opened the door and informed him that she'd left during the night, leaving a note for Jake. It hadn't said much, just where she was going and that she'd be back as soon as she could. It didn't take a genius to figure out what she had planned. The question was, what should he do now?

He should just let her get on with it and get back to his own job. She was a highly trained detective, as she'd been so eager to remind him. It wasn't his fault that she was too damn impatient.

Banging his fist on the steering wheel of his car which was still in the driveway of the house, he cursed. He knew he wasn't going to let her do this alone and it irritated the hell out of him that he couldn't just walk away.

From what she'd told him the night before, Jamie was on the streets and you didn't need to be an L.A. detective to know that wandering the streets at night looking for someone was not the safest, or smartest, thing to do. He knew she'd argue that she didn't need a man to protect her but, whether she liked it or not, it was much more dangerous for a woman alone. *He didn't have a choice, really, did he?*

Putting his car in drive, he headed home. He'd need to pack a few things, not that he was planning on being away long, and make a couple of calls. He needed to let his boss know what was happening and he should call Carla and let her know, too.

He'd been dating Carla for about six months now. She owned the local hair salon and they'd met at a mutual friend's barbeque, hitting it off right away. He wasn't looking for anything long term, and he'd made that plain to her at the start, but recently things had been getting more and more committed. She spent most nights at his house now and he'd noticed more and more of her things left behind after each visit. He hadn't brought the subject up yet as he wasn't sure about his own feelings about it, but he knew the time was coming when he would have to make a decision about their future.

For now, though, he didn't have time to worry about it. Getting the all clear from his boss, he threw a few things into a gym bag and headed out the door. If she'd left in the middle of the night, she would have arrived early this morning. That meant, he hoped, that she wouldn't have had chance yet to actually get out onto the streets. If he made good time, he could be there by late afternoon.

Twenty-Nine

The noise from the street outside woke her. Glancing at her watch, she realized with a start that she'd been asleep for several hours and it was now late afternoon. Sitting up, she raised her hands above her head and stretched, her body tense after lying in the same position for a long time.

Padding over to the hotel room window, she pulled the curtains aside, letting in the last of the afternoon sun. The streets were full of people going about their business. Somewhere out there was her niece, and she wasn't going home until she found her.

Knowing that she had a long night ahead of her, she decided to shower and then go and have something to eat. Her stomach was reminding her that she hadn't eaten that day and she needed to re-fuel.

She was just about to step into the shower when she heard a loud buzzing. Curious, she slipped on the hotel's courtesy robe and stepped back into the bedroom, realizing it was her cell, vibrating silently on the bedside table.

Picking it up, she noted that she had twenty-five missed calls and several voice mail messages. She must have been in a really deep sleep as the buzzing hadn't woken her up. Pressing the button to listen to the messages, she soon realized each one was from Finn and he sounded increasingly pissed in each one. The last of the messages had been left just now and in it he told her that if she didn't call him back he was headed straight to the police to report her as a missing person.

Annoyed, she sat back down on the bed and dialed the number on the screen.

"About damn time!" he barked at her as soon as he picked up. "Where the hell have you been? I've been trying to get hold of you since lunchtime!"

"I'm sorry, since when do I answer to you?" She was pleased that he'd called, but who did he think he was talking to her like that? "And where did you get my number from anyway?" She could hear him take a deep breath down the line.

"I'm sorry if I shouted. I've just been worried because I've been trying all afternoon and you didn't pick up. I stopped by the house this morning and Carrie gave it to me, along with your note."

"I've been asleep. I drove through the night and needed to catch up. My phone's been on vibrate."

"Well, if you had waited for me instead of dashing off in the middle of the night you wouldn't have had to drive through the night, would you?"

He had a point, but there was no way she was admitting it. "Well, it doesn't matter anyway. I did and I'm here now. What do you want, anyway?"

"Where are you now?"

"In a hotel. I'm just going to shower then have something to eat and start looking."

"What hotel?"

What was this? Twenty questions? "A Holiday Inn near the police station. Why?"

"Just go and have your shower. I'll talk to you later."

And with that she was left holding the phone to her ear, listening to the dial tone. *What was that all about?*

Shrugging it off, she showered quickly, not wanting to waste any time, and got dressed in fresh clothes.

The knock on the door made her jump and as she opened the door she was stunned to find Finn standing there. She was speechless and didn't know what to say as he walked through the open door and past her, into the room.

"This is nice," he said, looking around the room.

"What are you doing here?" She finally found her voice, though it sounded a bit croaky to her own ears.

"You didn't really give me much choice, did you, Kat?"

He stood there casually, hands in his pockets, but she could tell he was really mad. His eyes were almost burning through her and she had to look away.

"Why? I can do this on my own. I don't need a babysitter."

"Look, you came to me for my help, remember? And that's what I'm here for. To help. If you had waited instead of going off half-cocked, we could have come up together."

"I'm sorry. I just needed to do something. I'm not very good at being patient."

"So I see. Anyway, I'm here now. I've booked the room next door so, unless you've eaten in the last twenty minutes, I suggest we go and get something to eat and decide what we do next."

Nodding her agreement, she followed him out of the room to the elevator. She didn't want to admit it, but she was pleased he was here. Between them, they would find her. She just knew it.

Thirty

He'd grabbed her from behind. She'd never even heard him coming. Business had been quiet on her usual corner and she'd been using a shortcut through a vacant lot to try her luck somewhere else when he'd struck.

The darkness of the alley enveloped her as she was dragged further in, the street lighting gradually fading.

He had one hand clamped over her mouth so tightly she could feel her skin bruising. His skin was rough and it scratched against her as she tried to shake her face free. His other arm was wrapped around her waist, clamping her arms to her sides. God, he was strong. His grip felt like a vice and try as she might, she could not wriggle free.

This must be what the other girls felt. There was no doubt in her mind that this was the man. The man that they were all so scared of.

She'd lost her shoes and now she could feel her bare feet being torn as they scrambled for footing on the alleyway's floor. *She was going to die.*

She didn't want this to be her last memory. She didn't want the smell of oil from his fingers to be her last smell. Hot tears fell from her eyes and down her cheeks, onto her assailant's hand.

"You're a pretty one," he whispered, his breath hot in her ear. "What am I going to do with you?"

Panic rose in her throat and threatened to choke her, and she tried again to wrench her mouth free of his grip.

"Now, now, settle down. There's no point fighting it. All the others tried and look what happened to them?" His voice was deep and throaty and confirmed her worst fears.

Thinking of the other girls who'd been murdered at his hands, she felt her panic dissipate, replaced instead with a determination not to go down without a fight. Managing to open her mouth slightly, she pushed her teeth against his hand and sank them into his palm.

"Bitch!" he cried, trying to jerk his hand away, but she wouldn't let go. The copper taste of blood filled her mouth as she sunk her teeth deeper still.

The arm around her waist loosened and she grabbed her chance. Letting go of his hand and spitting the blood out of her mouth, she wrenched away from him and started running. Stumbling in the dark on torn and bloody feet, she didn't get very far before he was on her, grabbing her and bringing her crashing to the ground.

Her face pressed into the gravel she saw him pick up a brick near her head. "Take this, bitch," she heard, an instant before it made contact with the side of her head and her jaw went slack as she crumpled to the ground.

Thirty-One

"So what's life like on the LAPD?" he asked, as he reached for a breadstick.

They'd found an Italian restaurant not too far from the hotel and were now seated at a table in the back. It was a typical Italian place, with empty Chianti bottles hanging from the ceiling, red and white checked tablecloths and old black and white photos of Italy hanging all around. The walls were painted dark red and that, combined with the low lighting, made the atmosphere warm and inviting. Almost romantic, if you were on a date. Which she most definitely was not, she reminded herself.

"It's good. Tough, incredibly busy, but very satisfying."

"And they're okay about you taking all this time off?"

"I'm owed a lot of vacation time."

"I guess you'll be headed back there when this is all over?"

She looked at him, trying to see if there was any more to the question, but he just looked back at her openly, no hint that he cared either way.

"Yep." She nodded. "Assuming we find Jamie and can bring her home, then yes, that's the plan."

He just nodded and made no comment.

Their food arrived, and they ate in silence for a few minutes. Kat was starving and had ordered the lasagne. She dug in and didn't stop until she had satisfied the worst of her hunger pangs. Putting her fork to one side, she took a sip of water and sat back in her chair.

"I'll be honest. I'm not sure where to start. I don't have much of a plan."

"Well, what were you going to do before I arrived?"

"The video footage was taken at the scene of the murder of one of the local prostitutes. I checked online and found out that the murder took place about ten blocks from here. It got a lot of coverage because they think it's the work of a local serial killer." She took another drink of water. The lasagne was delicious, but far too salty. "I thought I'd just head over to that area with a picture of Jamie that I brought with me and see if anyone recognizes her."

She'd expected him to laugh but was surprised when he nodded slowly. "Good place to start. Certainly there's not much else we can do tonight, so I agree. That's what we should do. If we don't have any luck, we can make a new plan."

The rest of the meal was filled with small talk, Kat not wanting to bring up the past. Finn filled her in on what had happened to some of the others that they'd hung around with in high school, and she found herself relaxing and enjoying his company. For her part, she told him about her unauthorized trip to London with

Kyle and more about her job, but she didn't touch on the early days right after she'd left. There would be a time and place for that, and it wasn't now.

After eating their fill and settling the check, they decided to walk rather than take the car. It would be a good way to get a feel for their surroundings and the night was dry and clear. They'd been walking in companionable silence for a few minutes before he spoke.

"Did you ever think of me after you left?"

The question took her by surprise. She had thought about him. Almost every day at first. Over time, the yearning to come home had passed and the sorrow she'd felt when she thought of him had turned to curiosity about what he had done with his life. "Yes, I did." She answered truthfully.

They carried on walking, not looking at each other, and Kat waited for more questions to come but none did.

As they grew closer to their destination, the streets around them change. Gone were the upscale businesses and well kept residential townhouses, replaced by shops protected with steel bars across the windows and rundown buildings in various stages of disrepair. The sidewalks were no longer busy with people walking about purposefully going places; now the street corners were filled with groups of people just watching them as they walked past, tracking them with their eyes.

"I think this is as good a place as any to start." Kat eyed the prostitutes that had started appearing. "Here." She handed Finn one of the photos of Jamie that she had brought with her. "You start on that side of the street and I'll do this one."

She knew this wasn't going to be easy. In her experience, working girls were naturally suspicious and didn't like talking to strangers. But they might get lucky, and this was what she was counting on.

As she approached the first group of three girls on her side of the street, two immediately peeled off before she could reach them. One remained, though, looking defiantly at her as she approached.

"Hi, I hope you can help me. I'm looking for someone, my niece. Would it be okay if I showed you a photo?"

The girl just shrugged so, taking this as a yes, Kat showed it to her. She kept a close eye on her face as she took in the image, but there was no sign of recognition and with a shake of her head, the girl just turned and walked off.

She carried on all the way down the block, showing the photo to anyone she could get to look at it, but no one seemed to recognize Jamie. Hoping that Finn had had better luck, she waited for him at the end of the block and watched as he spoke to the last group of girls on his side before thanking them and turning to walk towards her.

"Any luck?"

"No, no one recognized her and I'm pretty sure they weren't lying."

Kat nodded. "Yeah, same on my side. But it's only the beginning," she said, making herself sound positive. It was still very early; they had the whole night ahead of them and a lot of ground to cover.

Fueled by coffee at every opportunity they got, they canvassed street after street, growing increasingly despondent and tired. Most people they approached were simply unwilling to even look at the photos and those that were had nothing to offer.

"Someone must know her!" Kat's feet were hurting, so she sat on the edge of a wall by an abandoned lot, sipping what must have been her tenth coffee since they'd set off. Thankfully, there was no shortage of corner shops open all night to keep them supplied.

"Maybe we should call it a night and come back tomorrow, after speaking to the police again."

"No, we're here now. We may as well keep going for as long as we can." Kat blew on her coffee to cool it down, looking at Finn over the rim. She desperately wanted to ask him about the woman she'd seen at his house but it really was none of her business.

"So, you joined up as soon as you left school?" She wanted to know more about his life since she'd left. She'd heard bits and pieces from her sister, but she wanted to learn more.

He laughed. "No, not right away. They wouldn't have taken me."

At her raised eyebrow, he elaborated. "I got into some trouble, went off track for a bit." Although he didn't say it, she knew that this was not long after she left. "Thankfully, Chief Finlay made it his mission to take me under his wing and he soon got me straightened out." He sighed. "If it weren't for him, I'd probably be in jail right now."

"You never wanted to move away? Maybe join a bigger department?"

He shook his head. "No, never. I love it where I am and there is plenty of crime going on to keep us busy."

He'd barely finished his sentence when the wail of sirens drowned him out. They watched as three squad cars turned onto the block and sped past before turning right at the end of the street. The sirens abruptly stopped, and looking towards the end of the street, they could see that they must have stopped just around the corner as the red and blue flashing lights were still visible.

Looking at each other without a word, they both dropped their coffees in a trash can and instinctively ran towards them.

As they rounded the corner, an ambulance sped past them, arriving on the scene just before they did.

They watched as the paramedics ran into an alley but were prevented from getting any closer by an officer standing at the entrance, keeping people out.

Though she had no authority there, she held up her badge to him, hoping that he wasn't the territorial type you sometimes came across.

"What's going on?"

He looked at the badge, then over his shoulder to make sure he wasn't overheard. "Looks like that serial killer has struck again, but this time he must have been disturbed or something because she's still alive."

Kat's heart sank. Another attack. All the more reason for her to find Jamie quickly and get her out of there.

By now, a crowd had started to gather, including several of the working girls, and Kat scanned the faces in the vain hope that she would spot her.

"Kat, come on, let's go. There's no point standing around here. We need to keep looking." He put his arm around her shoulders and squeeze her to him. "Don't worry. We'll find her."

The paramedics were wheeling the victim out of the alley now and Kat turned for a last look before leaving and froze.

"Jamie!" she cried, pulling away from Finn and dashing towards the stretcher before being caught and held back by one of the police officers now keeping the crowd at bay. "Finn! It's Jamie!"

"Let her go. It's her niece!" Finn explained to the officer who was struggling to hold on to her. His relief visible, he let her go and she ran to the stretcher.

"Oh, God, Finn, are we too late?" Kat's voice cracked as she looked at the pale woman lying unconscious on the stretcher, the blood from a head wound caking her hair into a red, sticky mess.

Thirty-Two

Kat had traveled in the ambulance with Jamie and Finn had gone back to the hotel to get his car and had joined her there. She'd been very lucky by all accounts, suffering a nasty head wound and cuts and scratches to her feet, but no other injuries.

They'd taken it in turns, giving statements to the local police who had now gone to continue the search for her assailant, leaving one officer behind in case she woke up. From what they'd been told, it appeared that Jamie was very nearly the victim of the serial killer hunting local prostitutes and it was only the fact that he'd been disturbed by one of them choosing that alley to service her client that had saved her life. He'd run off, leaving her there before he'd had the chance to do any serious damage.

Finn had gone to grab them some coffee from the cafeteria and he stood now, with the two steaming cups in his hands, watching them both through the glass window of the private room where Jamie lay. She had yet to regain consciousness but, for now, the doctors were not worried. She'd undergone numerous tests and scans when she'd been brought in and all appeared well. She would wake up in her own time, they'd said.

There were so many questions that needed answers but, for now, all that would have to wait. Pushing the door open with his hip, he handed Kat the hot drink. "Any change?"

Taking one of her hands away from the bed where she was gripping Jamie's, she took the cup from him with a small smile. "No, nothing yet." She took a sip of the coffee, grimacing at its bitterness. "Did you manage to call everyone?"

Finn sat down in the remaining chair. "Yes. I spoke to Jake and my boss and filled them in. Jake wanted to come straight here, but I've told him to stay there for the time being. When she's better, she will need to speak to the police, but for now everyone's just happy she's been found."

"You can head home now if you want. There's no need for you to stay." She said it quietly, keeping her eyes on Jamie and not looking at him.

"Do you want me to?"

She shrugged. "It's up to you. I'm going to stay with Jamie until she's well enough to come home, but you can't do anything else here. You may as well get back."

"No, I'll stay. If you don't mind, that is." He had no intention of going anywhere. He'd committed to bring this woman home and as far as he was concerned, his job wasn't over until that's exactly what he did.

"Of course, I don't mind." She smiled at him now. "Thank you, Finn, for everything."

Thirty-Three

She wasn't sure if her spine was ever going to be straight again. They'd pushed the two chairs in the room together and had taken turns sleeping on them while the other stayed awake, holding Jamie's hand and talking to her.

It had been two days now and she wasn't showing any signs of waking up yet. Stretching to get the kinks out of her back after her turn on the chairs, she looked at Finn. He'd fallen asleep with his head on the bed, still holding Jamie's hand.

He was such a good man, exactly the kind of man she'd imagined he'd become when they were teenagers. The thought made her sad, imagining what could have been if she'd stayed. He was breathing deeply and before she could stop herself, she reached forward and brushed a stray strand of hair from his forehead. She hadn't meant to disturb him but his eyes flickered and opened, and he raised his head from the bed.

"Everything okay?" His voice was still thick with sleep.

"Yes. I was just going to do a coffee run. Can I grab you one?"

"Mm, yes, please. My mouth feels like the bottom of a bird cage."

Just then, she caught a movement out of the corner of her eye. "Wait, did you see that?"

"See what?" he said, sitting up straighter.

"I saw her move. I'm sure I did." They both sat and watched, but nothing happened. Then, just as she was thinking it must have been wishful thinking, she saw it again. "There! Her hand moved!"

"You're right, it did."

Leaning across the bed so that she was close to Jamie's face, she tried to wake her up. "Jamie. Jamie, wake up, darling. It's Kat." Nothing, but she wasn't about to give up that easily. "Jamie, come on darling. It's time to wake up. Please, darling." She watched as her eyes flickered and slowly opened, eventually focusing on Kat's face. "Oh, God, thank you. We've been so worried about you."

Jamie looked at her, appearing confused. "Water," she croaked through dry lips.

"Of course, sorry!" Looking around, she saw that Finn was way ahead of her and had already poured a cup of water from the jug by the bed, holding it out to her. Taking it from him, she gently put her hand behind Jamie's head and lifted it from the pillow, holding the cup of water to her lips. After a few sips, Jamie laid back down with a sigh.

Turning her eyes to Kat once again, she spoke. "I'm sorry, who are you?"

It must be the knock to the head, Kat thought to herself. "It's me, Auntie Kat."

Jamie winced as she shook her head. "I'm sorry, but I've no idea who you are."

Worried now, Kat turned to look at Finn, who indicated that she should follow him outside. Nodding, she turned to Jamie. "You just rest, darling, we'll be back in a minute."

Leaving the room, neither of them spoke until the door was firmly closed behind them. "What's wrong with her? Why doesn't she recognize me?" The anguish was plain in her voice.

"I don't know, Kat, but we need to let the doctors know she's woken up. Maybe they can find out what's wrong."

"Okay. You go and do that. I'm going to stay with her." Watching him go, she took a deep breath and put a big smile on her face. She wasn't going to let Jamie know she was worried, and went back into the room.

***

"What are they doing in there?"

"Just come and sit down. They'll tell us soon enough."

She couldn't sit down, though. She'd been pacing back and forth outside the room for half an hour now, stopping every now and then to look through the window and see what was going on. So much so that one of the doctors had reached across and closed the blinds.

Just then, the door opened and the two doctors came out of the room.

"Is she okay? What's wrong with her?"

One of the doctors, the senior one judging by the way the other one held back, raised his hands and smiled. "One question at a time, okay?"

He pulled up a chair across from them in the corridor and sat down. "Well, physically I'm very pleased to say she's fine. There are no lasting effects from the blow to the head she received. She's been very lucky."

Relief flooded through her as she listened.

"But she does appear to have amnesia."

"What?" Kat was confused. "I thought you just said that the blow hadn't done any physical damage?"

The doctor smiled patiently at her. "It didn't. She doesn't remember how, but about a year and a half ago she remembers waking up, injured, in a forest. She has no memory of anything before that. Unfortunately, the only memories she has are ones since that time."

Thirty-Four

Coming Home

It felt strange. She was going to a place she didn't remember, with people she didn't know. But in an inexplicable way, it also felt familiar.

When she'd woken up in the hospital, her first thought was that she wasn't dead, after all. Somehow, she'd survived the attack. She'd thought the strange woman talking to her had been one of the doctors and she'd been utterly confused when she'd kept calling her Jamie and said she was her aunt.

Once she'd told the doctors about her amnesia and she'd undergone a battery of tests, she'd been told that physically she was fit and well and was free to leave. But go where?

The woman called Kat had explained that she was her aunt and that she'd been missing from a town three hundred miles away for well over a year and that they'd almost given up hope of finding her alive. It was a chance broadcast on the news that had led them to her.

She welcomed the idea of not going back to Blade, of having the better life she'd imagined countless times. Kat had been horrified when she'd found out that she thought she was wanted for murder and had quickly assured her that it was all lies. She would need a bit of time though, to adjust and to get used to the idea that she wasn't who she thought she was at all.

She'd asked them to give her a couple of days to think things through and they'd willingly agreed, checking her into the same hotel where they both had rooms. She'd spent a lot of time on her own, just thinking, but she'd also spent some time with them and had decided that, if they were terrible people, they were doing a very good job of hiding it.

Finally she'd made a decision and now, here she was, in the car with Kat headed back to the place she'd once called home. Finn was following behind in his own car, so it gave them some time alone together and Jamie was using it to try and find out as much as she could.

The news that both her parents had died weeks before she'd been found was devastating. She couldn't remember them so her grief was tempered, but there was no denying that it was still there.

Kat had been insistent that she didn't return to her apartment and had taken her to the mall to get anything that she needed. The comfortable slacks and t-shirt she was wearing now felt much better than the revealing clothes she'd been used to wearing. She'd wanted to go back for her money, but Kat wouldn't let her, explaining that she was quite wealthy and didn't need it. That had made her slightly uncomfortable; she'd worked so hard to save it, but then she realized if she was leaving that life behind, then she needed to leave it all behind.

"Can you tell me a bit more about my brother?" she asked now.

"Sure. Jake's only a few months older than you because he was adopted just before your mom found out she was expecting you. The two of you are really close."

"I can't wait to meet him." And it was true, she was excited and nervous all at the same time.

"Well, not long now. We're only about half an hour away."

***

There had to be some mistake, she thought to herself as they drew closer to the beautiful house which appeared at the end of the driveway. *I would have remembered a place like this!* Wouldn't she? Kat had told her what to expect, but actually seeing it was something else.

Her nerves were really kicking in now and she bit her bottom lip nervously. She had no idea how to deal with this. The doctors had told her to take things slowly, just one step at a time. They'd found no medical reason for her amnesia, so they'd told her that she must have suffered some sort of trauma, which seemed likely given what she did remember. Her memory could come back today, tomorrow or never.

She wasn't sure which she preferred, having no idea what the trauma was that she was blocking out but this, this was the strangest thing she had ever experienced.

"Don't worry, you'll be absolutely fine." Kat said gently. The car had come to a stop and she hadn't even noticed.

"What if I don't remember?" She didn't know how to behave. She was scared that they would think her odd.

"It doesn't matter if you do or you don't. Jake is your family, your brother. He loves you, and has missed you horribly. He won't care if you remember him or not, he's just glad you're coming home."

Coming home. All this time, she'd had a home to come back to and she hadn't known. Blade had preyed on her when she was at her most vulnerable, feeding her a pack of lies about what she had supposedly done. She'd been too trusting, too scared to doubt what he said. The anger she'd felt toward him when Kat had told her the truth had been all consuming; she'd wanted to find him, lash out. The time for that would come another day, though. For now, she was home.

Thirty-Five

For the first time in years, since she was a kid still living in the trailer park, Carrie was actually terrified. When Kat had called from the hospital telling them that they'd found Jamie, her knees had almost buckled under her. She forced herself to smile as Jake took her in his arms and swung her round the room, he was so happy. Her insides had been roiling though. *How was it possible? It couldn't be!* They hadn't heard the whole story yet but whatever it was, this could only be bad news for her.

"They're here!" The excitement in his voice was palpable, but Carrie just felt sick.

"You go, I'll get out of your way." She had no intention of being there when Jamie walked through the door. What if she recognized her? She knew that she'd lost her memory but there was still a chance, right?

"Don't be silly. She's your family, too!" He went to take her by the hand and pull her towards the front door.

She couldn't make a scene; if she did, Jake would know something was up. Even he wasn't that stupid. But if Jamie remembered what she'd done, it was all over.

She'd considered running as soon as she'd heard Jamie had been found. She'd even started packing a bag.

But where would she go? And besides, there was no way she was walking away from everything she had here unless she had absolutely no choice.

In the end, she'd relied on the fact that if she hadn't gotten her memory back in all this time, she wasn't likely to get it back now. She just needed her to stay that way for long enough for her to put her plan into action.

"Ok, if that's what you want," she replied, allowing herself to be reluctantly pulled outside.

***

Jake couldn't understand Carrie's attitude. He'd never wanted to marry her in the first place, but what choice had he had? It was that or go to prison. It certainly wasn't love, they usually got along all right, but since the reading of the will she'd been unbearable. He'd expected her to be happier since the news had come that Jamie had been found. After all, that was what she wanted, to get her hands on his money and now she could. So why on earth was she behaving like this?

He wasn't going to worry about it right now, though. His sister was home. He'd been such a prick and hadn't realized until she went missing and his parents died just how much he loved them all. Even his dad. No more, though. From now on, he was going to be the perfect brother. He'd robbed her of her fiancé and he was going to do everything he could from now on to make it up to her.

Opening the front door, he rushed outside just as Jamie was climbing out of Kat's car. The rush of emotion he felt when he saw her brought tears to his eyes. Kat had warned him to take it slow, not expect too much, but he couldn't help himself. Closing the gap between them in a few strides, he enveloped her in a hug and held her to him.

"Oh, my God, I can't believe you're actually here." His voice was thick with tears as he spoke. "I've missed you so much."

"Let the poor girl breathe!" Kat had her hand on his arm and her face was wet with tears.

Suddenly, they were all hugging each other and laughing and crying at the same time.

"Jamie, this is my wife, Carrie." He indicated to where Carrie stood on the front steps of the house. "You have met, but we weren't married then."

"Nice to meet you, again." Jamie smiled as she walked up to Carrie and shook her hand.

"Come on, come inside." He put his arm around Jamie's shoulders.

"You coming, Kat?" he asked over his shoulder.

"I'll be there in a minute."

***

Kat watched as they walked into the house, her heart full to bursting. Finn had arrived shortly after they did and had stood apart while they said their hellos. She turned to him now.

"Thank you, for everything."

"Hey, I didn't do much. It was a lucky break, you catching that news broadcast. You didn't need me." He smiled.

"You were there for me." She smiled back. "That's much more than I deserve. Look, I've got to go in, but we need to talk. It's about time I gave you an explanation."

He shook his head. "It was a long time ago. Let's just leave it in the past and move on, okay? I've got to get back, too. I need to check in with my boss and fill him in. I gave him the basics on the phone but I need to give him a full report." He turned to get back into his car. "Jamie will have to make a statement, but I'm sure it can wait a couple of days until she's settled back in. I'll give you a call."

Kat watched as he drove off, then turned and walked into the house to join in the celebrations.

Thirty-Six

The next couple of days went by in a blur of photographs and news stories and it was all slightly overwhelming. She felt strangely at home in the company of these people, in this big house, even though she had no memory of it.

She had hoped that something would have struck a chord, unlocked that part of her mind that was keeping her life a secret from her, but there had been nothing. Not even a glimpse.

Jake and Kat couldn't do enough for her, and barely let her out of their sight. It was heart warming, if slightly claustrophobic. But for some reason, she just couldn't take to Carrie. There was something about her that made her uncomfortable and she'd found that she didn't like being left in a room alone with her. She'd caught Carrie staring at her a couple of times but she'd immediately looked away when Jamie had met her eyes.

She was looking forward to getting out of the house, though, albeit to the police station. Finn had called earlier that morning and asked if she would come into town and make a statement about what she remembered. It was the first time she was going out since she'd been back and was nervous about going alone, so she'd asked Kat to accompany her.

"You all set?" Jamie hadn't heard Kat come into the living room where she'd been sitting, enjoying the sunshine streaming through the windows.

"Yep, let's go and get this over with." She picked up her purse and followed Kat out to the car.

It only took them a few minutes to get to the police station and Finn was waiting for them outside when they pulled up.

"Hi, Jamie, how are you feeling?" He gave her a quick hug.

"I feel great. I just want to get this all put behind me now." She smiled.

"Of course. It won't take long. It's just a formality, really, unless you've remembered anything else?"

She shook her head. "No, I'm sorry. I wish I had."

"Don't push yourself. It'll come when it's ready. The receptionist will point you to the interview room. I just need a quick work with Kat, if that's okay?"

"No problem. I'll see you in there."

***

"What's up?" Kat asked curiously.

"Nothing. It's just been a couple of days since I've seen you and I wanted to know how you're getting along. Are you coping okay?"

"I'm fine. It's not easy at the moment but it will get better. And she's home, that's the main thing." She could tell that there was something else bothering him.

"Look, can I buy you dinner?"

Well, that was unexpected. She didn't know what to say. She'd enjoyed their dinner together in Parkway and that was exactly why she didn't think dinner together would be a good idea. "Do you mind if I take a raincheck?" she replied "It's just with Jamie and everything, it's just not a very good time right now."

"Sure, whenever. No problem." He climbed the steps. "I don't think this will take long, but I'll drop her home when it's done. Save you hanging around." He didn't wait for her to reply and pushed open the police station doors and was gone.

Thirty-Seven

It had taken a couple of hours to give her statement about what she remembered and everything that had happened to her since she'd disappeared. It was exhausting going through it all again, but it meant that she was one step closer to getting her life back. Finn had been waiting for her when she'd walked out of the interview room, having promised Kat he would make sure she got home safely.

"Could I ask you a favor?" They were headed back to the house but there was a detour Jamie wanted to make on the way.

"You can ask. I can't promise anything, though!" He took his eyes off the road and smiled at her.

"I want to go to the cemetery. I don't want to ask Kat because I don't want to upset her, but I need to see where my parents are, and Ted." Tears filled her eyes. "It's awful. I don't remember them, my own parents and the man I was supposed to marry. I just feel like I need to go."

"Are you really sure you're up to it? You've only been back a few days. Why don't you give it a bit longer?" he asked softly.

"No, I need to do this. Please."

He nodded. "Okay."

It only took them a few minutes to get there and, after telling her where she would find them, Finn stayed in the car, wanting to give her some privacy.

Picking her way across the grass, she visited her parents first. Kneeling in front of the headstones, she talked to them, telling them all about what she remembered and about how sorry she was that they weren't there to see her come home. She stayed there for about twenty minutes before standing up and heading over to where Ted was buried.

She'd been shocked when Kat had explained that he had been killed, presumed murdered, and that his killer had never been caught. Coming so soon as it did before her own disappearance, she'd questioned whether the two incidents were related but Kat had assured her that they'd found no connection, that it was just a tragic coincidence.

Resting her hand on his headstone, she said goodbye. She was just turning away when she was suddenly struck by a sharp, stabbing pain behind her left eye. It was so severe that it made her gasp out loud and she had to hold on to the headstone to stop herself falling to her knees. Making herself take deep breaths, she held her hand over her eye until the pain eventually receded enough for her to make her way back to the car where Finn was waiting.

He must have known something was wrong, because as soon as he saw her coming he leapt out of the car and came towards her.

"Are you okay? You look as pale as a ghost!" he asked, taking her by the elbow and guiding her to the passenger seat.

"I'm fine. I don't know what happened but I got a sudden pain. It's nearly gone now, though." Relieved to be sitting down, she rested her head back against the headrest. "I've probably just overdone it a bit today. I'll be okay when I've had a rest."

"Okay. Well, let's get you home and then Kat can decide whether or not we need to call the doctor."

"Honestly, there's no need. I'm fine now," she protested.

"We'll see. You've been through a lot. She'll probably just want to get you checked out."

She didn't bother arguing, knowing that she probably wouldn't win, so simply agreed. "Okay."

***

On the drive back home, she kept her eyes closed and her head rested back and by the time they pulled up outside the pain had almost completely dissipated. Finn had called ahead from the car and Kat was waiting anxiously for them on the front steps.

"Are you okay? What's wrong?" she said as she helped her out of the car.

"Please stop fussing, both of you! I'm fine, it was just a bit of a headache." She smiled. "Though it is lovely to have you both looking after me."

"I think I should call the doctor." Kat frowned, not looking convinced.

"Please don't. I promise you, if I thought I needed one I would, but I don't. I'm just going to go and lie down for an hour and rest. You'll see, it will be gone by the time I wake up."

"Well, if you're sure. I was going to head into the office and go over some things with Jake, but I'll stay here with you."

"Don't you dare. Is Carrie here?" Kat nodded. "Then you go. I won't be on my own and if I need anything, I'll ask her."

Thirty-Eight

She'd been wrong. The headache hadn't gone; if anything it had gotten worse. She'd fallen asleep shortly after lying down, setting her alarm so she didn't sleep for too long. She'd realized as soon as she'd moved to turn it off after it started buzzing that she hadn't gotten any better, sharp shards of pain stabbing at her head. It felt like a razorblade was ricocheting around in her skull.

Lying her head back down, keeping her eyes closed, she waited for it to pass. It didn't. Instead, images started to appear behind her eyelids. They were hard to make out at first, coming slowly. Gradually, though, they started coming faster and then faster still. The images were no longer just images now, though. Snippets of memories were coming into her head, a jumble of pieces that made no sense, sending her senses spiraling. It felt like a wave of information was suddenly been dumped in her brain, so much of it that it was overwhelming.

And then it stopped. As if someone had flicked a switch, all the pieces suddenly fell into place. She remembered everything.

The pain was gone completely, now. Opening her eyes, it took her a moment to get her bearings before sitting up on the bed. The emotion of the memories she had lost washed over her, and the full force of the grief from the loss of her parents suddenly hit, her heart ripping in two. She didn't have time to dwell, though, as more memories were assaulting her, coming thick and fast.

She remembered that night, remembered going to Carrie's place. Remembered leaving, remembered what she'd told her about Ted. More importantly, she now remembered who had attacked her.

Thirty-Nine

Her memory would come back one day, she was sure of it. The fact that it hadn't yet gave her a bit of time, a bit of breathing space to decide where to go from here. She was not leaving without money in her pocket, though, no way. She would not go back to her shitty life, scrambling around to make ends meet.

The question was, where did she go from here? She'd given it some serious thought. For the first couple of days after Jamie's return, she'd kept a low profile, staying out of the way. She hadn't wanted to do anything that would likely trigger a memory. But she was showing absolutely no sign of remembering anything so she was more relaxed about it now. But knew it could change at any minute.

Now that she was back though, the trust could be dissolved and all the inheritance released. And this was what she was waiting for. As soon as Jake got his share of the money, she was out of here, taking a big chunk of it with her.

That was going to take some time, though. So, for now, she just had to bide her time and keep her fingers crossed.

A creak in the ceiling told her that Jamie was up. They wouldn't have been so quick to leave her to look after her if they'd known the truth. It was quite hysterical, really.

Hearing footsteps on the stairs, she called out, "Are you feeling better? Can I get you anything?" Confused when there was no reply, she left the kitchen and walked into the hallway. Jamie was halfway down the stairs and she had to admit, she did look sick. She was as white as a sheet and she could see that she was trembling. "Are you okay?"

She just nodded. "I'm fine. I just need to go out for a minute."

"I'm supposed to be watching you and you don't look fine. I think you should stay here until Kat and Jake get home. Where do you need to go, anyway?"

Jamie wouldn't meet her eyes as she replied, "I just need to get some air."

Something was wrong here. Carrie took a step towards her and she visibly drew back, flinching. The smile fell from her face and all pretence at concern was lost.

"You've remembered." It wasn't a question, it was a statement. It was clear to see that she was terrified of her.

"I haven't remembered anything. I just don't feel very well and need a bit of air. I won't be long," she said, taking a step down the stairs.

Did she think she was stupid? Crossing the hall in a few steps, Carrie stood at the bottom of the stairs looking up at her. "Don't play with me, Jamie."

She could tell the moment she decided to stop pretending, and she raised her head and looked her directly in the eye.

"Why?"

"Why? You were on your way to tell your parents about me and Ted. They hated me already. If you'd told them that, it would have ruined everything."

"Ruined everything? What are you talking about? You didn't need their permission to get married!"

"No, but they would have certainly cut Jake out of their will if we'd gotten married without it. What would have been the point in that?" she snarled at her.

Jamie looked shocked. "All this has been about the money? That's why you married him?"

She laughed. "Don't look so surprised. It's all right for people like you. When have you ever wanted for anything? I don't suppose you went to bed hungry more often than not when you were a kid, did you?" She shook her head. "I didn't want to hurt you, really, but I was this close." She held up her forefinger and thumb. "This close to getting what I wanted and I wasn't about to let you ruin it."

"Does Jake know?"

"No, he doesn't have a clue. He's not that smart."

"So what are you going to do now? Kill me and run?"

"If I was going to run, I would have gone when we first got the phone call to say you'd been found. No, I'm not going anywhere without my money."

"You're nuts. They'll be home soon and when they walk through that door I'm telling them everything and you can go to hell."

"And take your brother with me." She smiled triumphantly at the confused look on Jamie's face.

"I thought you said he didn't know?"

"He doesn't. But you see, your darling brother is far from innocent himself. Unfortunately for him, he made the mistake of trusting me with his secret and if I go down, he's coming right along with me."

"What on earth are you talking about? What secret?"

She laughed, enjoying herself immensely. "Who do you think killed Ted?"

"You're lying!"

She shook her head. "No, I'm not. Oh, he didn't mean to, it wasn't murder or anything, just a terrible accident. But after all this time, who's going to believe that? And if you tell anyone about me, well, you'll be sending your own brother to prison, too."

She watched as what she said hit home and Jamie lowered herself to sit on the stairs.

"I don't think you want to do that, do you?"

***

She felt sick. It was too much. Her own brother had killed Ted? Why? Why would he do that to her? And more importantly, what did she do now?

Carrie was stood at the bottom of the stairs grinning, knowing she'd won.

"What do you want?"

"I want you to keep your mouth shut. I just want the money, that's it, and I'll be gone. Once the will is settled, I'll siphon off a chunk and then I'll be gone and you can go back to your sad little life with your pathetic brother and you'll never have to see me again."

What choice did she have? She didn't know what had happened with Ted, but Jake was her brother, he was all she had left. She couldn't be responsible for sending him to prison.

"Okay. You win."

"Of course I do, I've got all the cards. Now, go back upstairs like a good girl and practice acting like you've lost your memory. No one can find out that it's come back or they'll start asking questions and you know what happens then, don't you?"

Jamie knew exactly what she was saying and did as she was told, turning and walking back up the stairs.

Forty

The Pontiac's magic wasn't working today. He'd finished his shift and headed straight home, looking forward to shutting the world out. Unfortunately, it wasn't happening. He'd been in the garage for nearly two hours and had gotten very little done to show for it. Most of it had been spent lying on a dolly underneath it, staring into space.

He'd been telling the truth when he'd told Kat that very little had any meaning after she'd left. Yes, they'd only been kids, but even then he had known that this was the woman he wanted to spend his life with. He'd had no desire to be like all the other guys who were running around on their girlfriends; it just hadn't interested him. He'd had everything he wanted in Kat.

He would never forget the day he'd found out she'd gone. Her father had told him in no uncertain terms that she wouldn't be coming back and to get over it. He'd tortured himself for months, replaying every conversation, trying to see if there was any sign that it had been coming. He'd been convinced that somehow it had been his fault, something he'd done.

Eventually he'd gotten past it, but it had taken a long time and there was still a part of his heart that was permanently scarred. It was getting harder and harder to pretend that he didn't care about it, though. All this time spent in her company had just made him remember how good they'd been together and he knew that he needed answers now. He needed to know what had made her leave.

Pushing himself out from underneath the car, he was just pulling himself to his feet when the door to the kitchen opened. *Damn, he'd forgotten Carla was coming over!*

"Hi, sweetie!" She reached up to kiss him.

"Hey." He replied, his tone less than enthusiastic earning him a pout. "Sorry, I'm just tired. Been working all day and I'm beat."

"You're forgiven." She turned and walked into the kitchen with him following behind. "Do you want me to cook?"

"Yeah, that would be good. I'll just go wash up." Leaving her busying herself in the kitchen, he went upstairs to shower and change. The smell of pasta wafted up the stairs as he dried himself off and he realized that he was starving.

"Smells good," he said, walking into the kitchen a few minutes later.

It was a warm night so they decided to eat on the back porch. Usually the conversation flowed, but tonight his mind was elsewhere.

"Finn? Finn, are you even listening to me?"

He realized she'd been talking to him but he hadn't heard a word she said. "I'm sorry. God, I must be more tired than I thought." He needed to get this straightened out. "Look, do you mind if you don't stay over tonight? I think I need a good night's sleep." Her face told him that she did mind, but he really needed to be on his own right now.

"You can't sleep with me here?"

How could he explain without hurting her feelings that he simply didn't want her there that night? "I just want a bit of time to myself. It's been a busy few days." He smiled to soften his words. "I'll see you tomorrow, okay?"

She still wasn't happy as he kissed her goodbye at the front door, but the minute the door was closed she was gone from his mind. Going back outside, grabbing his cell from the kitchen on the way, he dialed Kat's number.

"I was just wondering if you wanted to come over?" he asked when she picked up. The brief silence on the other end of the phone told him that she was thrown by his request, and he was sure she was going to refuse. He was surprised when she agreed.

***

He felt stupidly nervous. It wasn't like this was a date or anything. He just wanted to clear the air, get some answers, and maybe put what happened behind him once and for all. But for some reason, he felt like a teenager all over again. Perhaps it was because this was the first time they were meeting for reasons not related to Jamie.

By the time the doorbell rang a short time later, he'd washed up the dinner dishes and put some beers in the fridge to chill.

"Hi," he said as he opened the door. "Thanks for coming over." She stood in the glow of the overhead porch light with a bottle of red wine in her hands.

"Here," she said, handing it to him. "Thanks for inviting me."

They both just stood there for a moment, looking at each other. "Okay, why does this feel awkward?" He smiled at her.

She let out a soft laugh "I don't know. It does, though, doesn't it?"

"Come one, let's get this open." He held the door open for her to come in, closing it and taking a deep breath before following her through to the kitchen.

"How is Jamie doing?" he asked as he opened the bottle to let it breathe.

"She's doing okay, I think. I haven't been home since I saw you earlier. There was so much to go over in the office and then I had to go into town to see the lawyer again now that she's been found. Jake and Carrie are there, though, and I've told them to call me if there are any problems."

Picking up the bottle and two glasses, Finn gestured her to follow him out onto the porch. "So what are you going to do now, head back to L.A.?" He didn't look at her while he waited for the answer, focusing on pouring the wine. He wasn't sure he wanted to hear the answer.

"Not right away, no. The paperwork over the estate will take a little time, but I don't need to be here for that. I don't want to leave just yet, though, not until I'm sure that Jamie is going to be okay."

He was surprised. He thought she'd be eager to get back as soon as possible. "You don't sound like you like the idea too much."

"It's just that over the past few days I've realized how much I've missed out on all these years, and I don't want to miss out on any more." She smiled at him. "I definitely won't be staying away as long this time."

"That's good to hear."

"Really? You mean that?"

"Of course. It would be great for them to have you around more." That wasn't the real reason, he knew that. It was good to hear because he found himself wanting to see a lot more of her.

As the wine was drained from the bottle, and then they started on the beer, they reminisced about their days in high school, leading to fits of laughter when they remembered the things they'd gotten up to. They were both enjoying the evening and purposefully stayed away from the subject of her leaving. After one particularly spectacular laughing fit, which nearly had Finn choking on his beer, they decided it might be time for coffee.

"I'll make it," Kat volunteered, and he leaned back on the kitchen counter happily watching her move about his kitchen. While the kettle boiled, she turned to him. "Thank you. It means more than you know that we're able to do this."

Maybe it was the alcohol or the relief of having found Jamie. Whatever it was, in that moment he couldn't stop himself. Crossing the gap between them in one step, he took her face in his hands, cupping it as he looked into her eyes. He'd expected her to pull away, but she didn't. Encouraged, he brushed her bottom lip with his thumb before leaning down and touching his lips to hers briefly.

Looking into her eyes, he searched for a sign to stop but there was none. Pushing his hand into the hair at the back of her head, he pulled her tightly to him, all restraint gone. He felt her lips part under his, welcoming him. Her hands pulled his shirt from the waistband of his jeans and slid up his bare back, pulling him close.

The shrill ringing of his cell was like an alarm bell in the silent kitchen, snapping them both out of the moment.

"Shit! I've got to see who that is in case it's work." Cursing, he quickly went to grab his phone from the porch. It was Carla. Feeling a brief stab of guilt, he returned to the kitchen but Kat wasn't there. "Kat?"

"I've got to go," she said from where she was standing by the front door.

"What? Why?" He was confused.

"This was a mistake. I'm sorry, Finn." She opened the front door to leave.

"What? Just like that you're walking out on me again with no explanation?" He hadn't meant for this to happen, but she had been as willing as he was.

Forty-One

"Are you okay?" Kat had told him that she wasn't feeling very well, but since he'd gotten home Jamie had hardly spoken to him and refused to meet his eyes.

"I'm fine. I just wish everybody would stop asking me that!" she snapped at him.

Carrie was acting strangely, too. She'd hardly taken her eyes of Jamie and even now, as they sat in the living room watching TV, her eyes were on her constantly.

"Have you two had a disagreement or something?" Okay, there was no mistaking it that time. They definitely exchanged a look. There was something they weren't telling him. "Okay, spit it out." He looked at each of them in turn, waiting for an answer.

"You're imagining things," Jamie told him, but she was looking at Carrie as she said it. With a sigh, he stood up. "Okay. Well, if you're not going to tell me I'm going to get myself a drink. Anyone want anything?"

"Yeah, could you make me a hot chocolate, the way you always made them, with marshmallows?"

It wasn't until he reached the kitchen that he realized what Jamie had just said. *She'd remembered!* But if that were true, why on earth hadn't she said anything? Maybe she was just remembering little things without even realizing it? All thoughts of a drink forgotten, he rushed back to the living room.

"Jamie! Do you realize what you just said?"

She looked confused. "What are you talking about?"

"You asked for a chocolate *the way I always used to make it!*" He was grinning now "You remembered something!" He'd been expecting her to be as excited as he was but he didn't see excitement in her eyes now, just naked panic.

"You stupid bitch!"

He whirled to face Carrie as she hissed this at Jamie. "What the hell?" He had no idea what was going on. "Will someone tell me what the hell is going on here?"

"Jake, just leave it alone. Please!" Jamie was pleading with him.

"No, I won't leave it alone! Something is going on here and I want to know what!" He turned to Carrie "Why did you say that?" She didn't reply, instead just looking at him in disgust.

"Okay, if neither of you are going to tell me, I'll call Kat. She can come home and straighten this out." He reached into his pocket for his cell phone.

"I wouldn't do that if I were you." He looked up from dialing the number to find Carrie standing in front of the TV, pointing a gun and him and Jamie.

"Drop the phone and kick it over here." In shock, he did what he was told.

"I should have known you were too stupid to pull it off," she snarled at Jamie.

"Carrie, what is going on? What the hell do you think you're doing?"

Keeping the gun trained on them, she sneered, "Your precious sister got her memory back this afternoon. Unfortunately, that meant she remembered who attacked her."

The confusion must have shown on his face. "Hasn't the penny dropped yet?"

"Oh, my God! It was you!"

"Well done. Give the boy a medal."

"Why on earth didn't you do the job right? If you had, we wouldn't be in this mess," he said to her, grinning.

"What? Are you kidding me?" She wasn't sneering any more.

"Jeez, if you'd told me what was going on I would have helped you! Dammit Carrie."

"What the hell are you taking about?"

"Well, I managed to get Ted out of the way. Did you think I'd have a problem getting rid of Jamie? She's not even my real sister, for God's sake!"

She looked unsure of herself now. "But you've been so worried about her, going on and on about finding her."

"Yeah, because I knew full well that if she was found I needed to keep the family in the dark. You know how much the money and the business mean to me. I don't give a crap about anything else. We'll be lucky to get away with anything, now."

"Jake, what are you saying! You can't mean this!" Jamie cried looking at him with wide, tear-filled eyes. "Oh, my God, Jake, this can't be happening." She dropped her face into her hands and started sobbing.

Marching over to stand in front of her, he pulled back his arm and slapped her with a backhand hard across the face. "God, I've been wanting to do that for years." He turned to Carrie. "We're screwed now. The best we can hope for is to get out of here." He held out his hand. "Give me the gun and I'll watch her. You go upstairs and get what you can. All my mother's jewelery is still in her room and Jamie's got some nice stuff, too."

"You must think I'm an idiot," Carrie said, her brow wrinkled. "You go and get the jewelery and I'll stay here and watch her," she said, waving toward Jamie with her gun.

He shrugged. "Okay, but don't screw it up this time." Without looking at where Jamie was sitting, holding the side of her face, he turned and left the room."

As soon as he was clear of the living room he quickened his pace and headed upstairs to his parents' room. She'd taken his cell so he couldn't call Kat or Finn because he didn't know their numbers as they were programmed in his phone. He considered calling 911, but dismissed that thought almost immediately. They might not get here in time, and if Carrie heard them coming, she'd know that there was no escape and a cornered wild animal will do anything, including kill Jamie. No, he had no choice. It was on him.

He knew that his dad had kept a gun in his bedside table and he just hoped to God it was still there. *Yes!* He let out a breath as his hand closed around the cold metal of the gun in the bottom drawer. Checking that it was loaded, he took a deep, steadying breath. Grabbing his mom's jewelery box, he headed back downstairs. This had gone on long enough. It ended now.

Forty Two

What had she been thinking? She hadn't been thinking, that was the problem. If she had, she would never have gone to Finn's. At night. With a bottle of wine.

She'd hoped that after everything that had happened over the last few days, they would be able to come to some kind of a truce. She needed that. She hadn't truly realized until she'd come back just how much her past still weighed her down. She certainly hadn't expected to find herself in his arms once again. Oh, she was still attracted to him. She'd realized that the first day, but she'd had no idea he felt the same way.

It would be different if he knew the truth and still felt the same way, but he didn't and she couldn't deceive him like that. No, she would just have to avoid seeing him until she left. It wouldn't be long now, and then she could get back to her life. That thought had held such appeal just a few short days ago but now, for some reason, she was dreading it more and more.

Forty-Three

"I've got it," he announced, walking back into the living room. He'd concealed the gun in the waistband of his jeans, in the small of his back. Now he just needed to wait for the right time. "What now?"

"We go. Before Kat gets back. With any luck, we'll get a bit of a head start."

He nodded over at Jamie. "What do we do with her?"

"If it wasn't for her, I'd have everything I want right now. I've got no intention of letting her enjoy what should have been mine. This time, I'll make sure she's dead."

How had he not known he'd married a monster? He'd known she was tough when he'd first met her, and he'd discovered she was ruthless when he'd told her about killing Ted and she didn't bat an eye, but this? He'd never even considered that she might have had anything to do with Jamie's disappearance. *He was such an idiot!* But one thing he did know was that he had started all this, he had brought this monster into their family, and now it was up to him to deal with it.

Turning her back on him, she raised her arm and pointed the gun at Jamie. It was now or never.

"Put the gun down, Carrie," he said, his voice surprisingly calm.

Keeping the gun trained on Jamie, she turned her head and looked at him. "You bastard. I should have known. Killing Ted was one thing, but you really are soft when it comes to her, aren't you." She shook her head. "Such a shame. I was starting to think you had potential."

"You know damn well that killing Ted was an accident. I never meant for it to happen. My mistake was not coming clean at the time and letting you get your claws into me. A mistake I intend to rectify right now." His voice hardened. "Now put the gun down, Carrie. It's over."

He could see her turning her options over in her mind and realizing that she had none. He wouldn't put it past her to kill Jamie anyway and his finger tightened on the trigger, watching for the slightest sign that she was going to shoot.

She didn't, though, and after a tense few seconds, raised her hands. "At least I'll have the satisfaction of knowing you're going to prison with me."

He didn't reply, keeping his eyes on her but addressing Jamie. "Grab the gun."

He watched as she stepped forward and took the gun from Carrie's hand before handing it to him. He tucked it in his jeans before telling Jamie to go and call 911 on the house phone.

She didn't move, though. "Are you sure?" she asked him, a hard edge to her voice.

Surprised, his eyes flicked to her. "What do you mean? Of course I'm sure."

"Answer me one question, truthfully."

"Now? Can't this wait?"

"No, it can't, so will you? Tell me the truth?"

"Yes, of course, what is it?"

"Was Ted's death an accident?"

He allowed himself to meet her eyes briefly. "Yes, absolutely."

"Then shoot her."

"What? Are you nuts?"

"No. She tried to kill me. I lived through hell because of her. If you don't, you'll go to prison, too." She put her hand on his arm. "You did wrong, but you are all I have left and the only people who know are in this room."

For a moment, he allowed himself to consider what she was saying. It was true; if he shot Carrie now it would be easy to claim self-defense and no one would ever find out the truth about Ted. The moment quickly passed, though. He could never kill another human being in cold blood, and he knew in his heart that he needed to pay for what he'd done, accident or not.

"No, I can't do it Jamie. This all started because of my greed and I need to pay for what I did. I'm as responsible for what happened to you as she is." He gave her a small smile. "Go and call the cops, please."

"There's no need. I'll do it."

They both jumped at the sound of the voice. They could tell from the look on her face as she stepped into the room that Kat had heard everything.

"Oh, Kat, I'm so glad you're here!" Jamie flung herself into her arms.

"How long have you been standing there?" Jake asked her, meeting her eyes.

"Long enough to know that I'm proud of you for making the right decision."

He watched as she took her cell phone out of her pocket and dialed 911. All they had to do now was wait.

He didn't feel any panic as they waited for the police to arrive. Instead, he was filled with a sense of relief that it was all over and he had finally done the right thing. They all knew the truth now, and the fact that Jamie hadn't immediately condemned him made his heart soar, though he knew that he owed her answers.

She would be okay now. The monster that he married would spend the rest of her life in jail and she had Kat. That was all that mattered.

Forty-Four

Kat watched as first Carrie and then Jake were handcuffed and led away to the waiting squad cars, and was glad her sister wasn't there to see it. When she'd gotten home, she'd heard the voices coming from the living room. It wasn't until she got close that the conversation had stopped her in her tracks. Stunned, she'd stood there listening, while all the pieces clicked into place.

She'd held her breath as Jamie had told Jake to shoot, understanding her reasons but knowing it was wrong. Relief had washed over her when he had refused and, despite everything, she'd felt incredibly proud of Jake in that moment.

"What's going to happen to him?" Jamie asked her. They watched from the front steps as they were driven away.

Turning and going back into the house and closing the door behind her, she sighed. "He will go to prison, there's no doubt. How long will depend on what they decide to charge him with."

"I believe him, you know." Jamie said, following Kat into the living room where all the drama had taken place. "I mean, I believe him when he said that killing Ted was an accident."

Kat nodded. "Yes, I believe him, too. He's made mistakes, but he's not a bad man and he loves you dearly. He would never have intentionally wanted to hurt you."

"It was Dad. He made him the way he was. I remember it all now."

"Will you be able to forgive him?"

"I already have. He's suffered enough."

"And so have you." Kat took her in her arms. "I'm just glad it's all finally over and that you're safe at last."

They stood there for a while, just hugging each other both lost in their own thoughts.

Forty-Five

"I've been doing some thinking," Jamie said, breaking the silence. They'd both been caught up in their own thoughts since leaving the prison where they'd been to visit Jake.

He'd made a full statement to the police and there had been no doubt that he was totally ignorant of Carrie's attack on Jamie. They'd also accepted that what had happened to Ted had been an accident and that he'd never intended to kill him. The D.A. had offered him five years, which his lawyer had advised him to accept, avoiding the necessity of a trial. They'd both been very proud of the way he had handled it, stepping up to the plate and being not only willing, but wanting to take his punishment.

"Yeah?" Kat briefly took her eyes of the road and glanced over at her. "And what have you been thinking about?" It was finally over, but Jamie had a tough road ahead and Kat was worried about her.

"I'm on my own now. Well, for the next five years, anyway." She sighed. "It's too much. I've got to run the business, which I know nothing about, look after the house and Jake's affairs." He had signed over power of attorney to her before he was convicted.

"It's a lot to take on I agree, but I know you can do it." Kat tried to reassure her.

"Yes, I can. But I can't do it alone."

"Well, I can help you find someone suitable before I leave. Maybe we could speak to John Cassidy, the lawyer. He might be able to give us some recommendations."

Jamie shook her head. "No. I need someone I can trust completely. After everything I've been through, I need you, Aunt Kat."

She'd had a feeling that this was coming, had even been thinking about volunteering herself, but now that the question was out there she had no idea what to say. "Jamie, I've got a career, one I need to get back to."

It sounded empty even as she said it. More and more, lately, she'd been lamenting the fact that yes, she had a career, but very little else. And what was a life with nothing in it but work? She'd neglected her family while she still had one, and now that it had been torn apart, could she really just walk away?

"You could apply to the local PD, couldn't you?"

It's true, she could. But there was the small question of Finn. It was a small department, and if she did that it would mean working with him closely on a daily basis and she knew that that was something she simply couldn't do. She shook her head. "I'm sorry, Jamie, but no. That wouldn't work."

"Okay, well how about this then. You come and work for me? Now that we're taking on more sensitive projects, we need a security division and someone to head it up. You'd be perfect with your background. Will you please at least think about it?"

Kat nodded. Yes, she would think about it. "Okay, but I'm not making any promises."

Forty-Six

She was not looking forward to this conversation, but it was one that had been a long time coming.

She'd phoned Finn and they'd arranged to meet just outside town. When they were kids, they used to come to this spot to make out. It was one of the few elevated spots in an otherwise almost completely flat landscape, and from the top you could see for miles. She sat on the hood of her car waiting for him now, looking out over the town stretched out below her, bathed in the orange glow of the setting sun.

The sound of tires on dirt told her that he'd arrived. She gave him a small smile as he pulled himself up onto the hood to sit beside her.

"How's Jamie doing?" he asked, his voice filled with genuine concern.

"She's going to be fine. She's strong." She took a deep breath. "And I'm going to be by her side to help."

"You are?"

She could feel him looking at her, but she didn't turn to meet his gaze. "Yes. I've decided it's about time I came home." She sighed. "I should have come back sooner, been more of a sister, more of an aunt. I can't get that time back, but I can try and make up for it."

He nodded. "So, what are you going to do?"

She told him about the job Jamie had offered her, and that she'd decided to accept it.

"Is that what you brought me up here to tell me?"

This was it. It was time. "No, I brought you up here to tell you why I left all those years ago."

The End

Printed in Great Britain
by Amazon.co.uk, Ltd.,
Marston Gate.